The **Princess MIRROR-BELLE** Collection

Julia Donaldson is the author of many successful books for children, including *Room on the Broom* and the award-winning *The Gruffalo*. *The Gruffalo* has won the Smarties Prize and the Blue Peter Award for the Best Book to Read Aloud. Julia has also written many children's plays and songs, and runs regular storytelling and drama workshops. She lives in Glasgow with her family.

Lydia Monks studied Illustration at Kingston University, graduating in 1994 with a first-class degree. She is a former winner of the Smarties Bronze Award for *I Wish I Were a Dog* and illustrated *Sharing a Shell* by Julia Donaldson. Her illustrations have been widely admired.

Other books by Julia Donaldson

For younger readers
Brick-a-Breck
The Jungle House
The Quick Brown Fox Cub
Spinderella
The Wrong Kind of Bark

Novels
The Dinosaur's Diary
The Giants and the Joneses

Poetry
Crazy Mayonnaisy Mum

Plays
Play Time

A selection of picture books
Charlie Cook's Favourite Book
Fly Pigeon Fly *(with John Henderson)*
Follow the Swallow
The Gruffalo
The Gruffalo's Child
The Magic Paintbrush
Monkey Puzzle
One Ted Falls Out of Bed
The Princess and the Wizard
Room on the Broom
Sharing a Shell
The Smartest Giant in Town
The Snail and the Whale
A Squash and a Squeeze
Tiddler
Tyrannosaurus Drip
Wriggle and Roar

The Princess Mirror-Belle Collection
Julia Donaldson

3 books in 1

Illustrated by Lydia Monks

MACMILLAN CHILDREN'S BOOKS

Princess Mirror-Belle first published 2003 by Macmillan Children's Books
Princess Mirror-Belle and the Magic Shoes first published 2005 by
Macmillan Children's Books
Princess Mirror-Belle and the Flying Horse first published 2006 by
Macmillan Children's Books

This edition published 2008 by Macmillan Children's Books
a division of Macmillan Publishers Limited
20 New Wharf Road, London N1 9RR
Basingstoke and Oxford
www.panmacmillan.com

Associated companies throughout the world

ISBN 978-0-330-45398-1

3 5 7 9 8 6 4 2

A CIP catalogue record for this book is available from the British Library.

Printed and bound in the UK by CPI Mackays, Chatham ME5 8TD

Contents

Princess
MIRROR-BELLE

For Phoebe

Contents

Chapter One

DRAGONPOX

"You've got some new ones on your face," said Ellen's mum. "Don't scratch them or you'll make them worse."

Ellen was off school with chickenpox. She didn't feel all that ill but she *did* feel sorry for herself, because she was missing the school outing to the dolphin display.

"Can you read me a story?" she asked Mum. But just then the front door bell rang.

"I'm sorry, I can't. That's Mrs Foster-Smith come for her piano lesson. Look, here are your library books . . . and remember, *no scratching*." She went out of the room.

Ellen picked up one of the books. It was full of stories about princesses. She flicked through the pages, looking at the pictures. The princesses were all very beautiful, with swirly looking clothes and hair down to their waists. None of them had chickenpox. Ellen started to read *The Sleeping Beauty*, but it was difficult to concentrate. For one thing, her spots were so itchy. For another, Mrs Foster-Smith was thumping away at "The Fairies' Dance" on the piano downstairs. The way she played it, it sounded more like "The Elephants' Dance".

Ellen decided to have a look at her new spots. There was no mirror in her bedroom so she put on her right slipper (she had lost her left one) and padded into the bathroom.

She studied her face in the mirror over

the basin. One of the new spots was right in the middle of her nose. The more Ellen looked at it, the itchier it felt . . . Her hand crept towards it. Just a little *tiny* scratch wouldn't matter, surely. Her finger was just about to touch the spot when a strange thing happened. Her reflection dodged to one side and said, "Don't scratch or you'll turn into a toad!"

Ellen didn't reply. She was too surprised. She just stared.

"I've never *seen* such a bad case of dragonpox," said the mirror girl.

"It's not dragonpox, it's *chicken*pox,"

Ellen found herself saying. "Anyway, yours is just as bad – you're my reflection."

"Don't be silly, I'm not you," said the mirror girl, and to prove it she stuck one hand out of the mirror and then the other.

"Come on, help me out," she said, reaching for Ellen's hand.

Ellen gave a gentle pull and the mirror girl climbed out of the mirror, into the basin and down on to the bathroom floor.

"What a funny little room!" she said.

"It's not *that* little!" said Ellen. This was true – there was room in the bathroom for three of the tall pot plants that

Mum was so keen on.

The mirror girl laughed. "The bath-room in the palace is about ten times this size," she said.

"The *palace*?" repeated Ellen.

"Of course. Where would you expect a princess to live?"

"Are you a princess, then?"

"I most certainly am. I'm Princess Mirror-Belle. You really ought to curtsy, but as you're my friend I'll let you off."

"But . . . you don't *look* like a princess," said Ellen. "You look just like me. You've got the same pyjamas and just one slipper. You've even got a plaster on your finger like me."

"These are just my dressing-up clothes," said Mirror-Belle. "In the palace I usually wear a dress of silver silk, like the moon." She thought for a moment and then added, "Or one of golden satin, like the sun. And anyway, my slipper's on my *left* foot and my plaster's on my *right* finger. Yours are the other way round."

Ellen didn't see that this made much difference, but she didn't want to get into an argument, so instead she asked Mirror-Belle, "Why have you got the plaster? Did you cut yourself on the bread knife like me?"

"No, of course not," said Mirror-Belle. "I was pricked on my finger by a wicked fairy."

"Just like the Sleeping Beauty!" said Ellen. "Did you go to sleep for a hundred years too?"

"No – two hundred," said Mirror-Belle. "I only woke up this morning." She gave a huge yawn as if to prove it.

"Did you put the plaster on before you went to sleep or after you woke up?" asked Ellen, but Mirror-Belle didn't seem to want to answer this question. Instead she put the plug into the bath and turned on the taps.

"Hey, what are you doing?" asked Ellen.

"Getting the cure ready, what do you think?"

"What cure?"

"The cure for dragonpox, of course."

"But I haven't got dragonpox!"

"Well, I have," said Mirror-Belle, "and I'll tell you how I got it. I was in the palace garden last week, playing with my golden ball, when—"

"Weren't you still asleep last week?" Ellen interrupted. "Didn't you say you only woke up this morning?"

"I wish you'd stop asking so many questions. As I was about to say, an enormous dragon flew down and captured me. Luckily a knight came and rescued me, but when I got back to the palace I came out in all these spots. My mother the Queen sent for the doctor and he said I'd caught dragonpox."

"Well, my doctor said mine were chickenpox," said Ellen.

"I suppose you were captured by a chicken, were you?" said Mirror-Belle. "Not quite so exciting, really. Still, I expect the cure's just the same." She picked up a bottle of bubble bath and poured nearly all of it into the water.

"That's far too much!" shrieked Ellen. But Mirror-Belle was too busy investigating the cupboard on the wall to answer.

"This looks good too," she said.

"But that's my dad's shaving cream," said Ellen.

"It's nice and frothy," said Mirror-Belle, squirting some into the bath. "And *this* looks just the job," she said, taking the cap off a tube of Minty-Zing toothpaste, which had red and green stripes.

"Nice colours," said Mirror-Belle, squeezing most of the toothpaste out into the bath.

Ellen was a bit shocked at first but

then she giggled.

"Shall we put some of Luke's hair gel in too?" she asked. Ellen's big brother had started getting interested in his appearance recently and was always smoothing  bright blue sticky stuff into his hair.

"Good idea," said Mirror-Belle. Ellen scooped the gel out of the tube and into the bath. That would serve Luke right for all the times he'd hogged the hair-dryer.

Mirror-Belle poured in a bottle of orange-coloured shampoo and eyed the bath water thoughtfully. "We still need one more ingredient," she said. "*I* know!" She picked up Mum's bottle of Blue Moon perfume and began spraying merrily.

Ellen, who had begun to enjoy herself, felt rather alarmed again. Mum only ever put a tiny bit of Blue Moon behind her ears. By now the bathroom smelt like a flower shop.

"Let's get in now," said Mirror-Belle. In another moment the two of them were up to their chests in bubbles, cream, gel and toothpaste.

"I can feel the cure working already, can't you?" said Mirror-Belle, and flipped some froth at Ellen. Ellen flipped some back, and a blob of toothpaste landed on the spot on Mirror-Belle's nose.

Ellen noticed that Mirror-Belle, like herself, had a pale mark round one of her wrists.

"We've both got watch-strap marks," she said. "Did you lose your watch like I did?"

Mirror-Belle looked at her grandly and said, "This mark isn't from a *watch*. Oh no. It's from my magic wishing bangle."

"A wishing bangle! Can you wish for anything you want?"

"Naturally," said Mirror-Belle. "And for things that other people *don't* want."

"Such as?"

"Well, once I wished for a worm in the palace garden to grow to the size of a snake and give the gardener a fright."

"And did it?"

"Yes. The only trouble was, it didn't stop growing. It grew and grew till it took up the whole of the garden. Then we had to banish it to an island, but it *still* kept growing."

"But couldn't you just wish it small again?"

Mirror-Belle looked annoyed for a second but then her face cleared and she said, "No, because I dropped the bangle in the sea and it got swallowed by a fish. Luckily, though, I caught the

fish last week."

Ellen thought of reminding her once again that she had said she was asleep last week, but she decided not to. It would only make Mirror-Belle cross. It was more fun just to listen to her stories, even if some of them sounded a bit like fibs.

"I don't feel quite so bad about missing the dolphin display any more," she said.

"Is *that* all you're missing?" asked Mirror-Belle. "*I'm* missing the sea monster display."

The two of them played at being dolphins and sea monsters for a while, splashing a lot of water and froth out of the bath.

"Your dragonpox hasn't gone away yet," said Ellen.

"Don't be so impatient," said Mirror-Belle. "We haven't done Stage Two yet."

"What's that?"

"Get out and I'll show you," said

Mirror-Belle. They both got out of the bath and Mirror-Belle picked up a roll of toilet paper. She began winding it round and round Ellen, starting with her legs and working upwards.

"I feel like an Egyptian mummy," said Ellen, laughing.

Mirror-Belle reached Ellen's face. She wound the paper round and round until Ellen couldn't see out.

"Now you have to count to a hundred," she said.

"What about you?" asked Ellen.

"We'll do me later," said Mirror-Belle.

Ellen started to count. She could hear Mirror-Belle moving

about the room and from downstairs came the sound of Mrs Foster-Smith playing "The Babbling Brook". The way she played it, it sounded more like "The Crashing Ocean".

When Ellen got to about eighty she heard Mirror-Belle say something which sounded like, "Ow! Stupid old taps!"

When she got to a hundred she tried to unwind the toilet paper but it got into a tangle.

"Help me, Mirror-Belle," she said. But there was silence.

Ellen managed to tear the toilet paper away from her eyes, but Mirror-Belle was nowhere to be seen.

"Mirror-Belle! Where are you?" called Ellen. Mirror-Belle's pyjamas had disappeared as well. Could she have put them on and gone out of the room?

Ellen opened the door. Maybe Mirror-Belle had gone downstairs. Ellen was still half-wrapped in toilet paper but she didn't bother about that. She set off downstairs in search of Mirror-Belle.

When she was six stairs from the bottom, two things happened. Ellen tripped up and fell down the stairs, and Mrs Foster-Smith came out of the sitting room. Ellen went crashing into her, and Mrs Foster-Smith let out a shriek.

"Ellen! What *are* you up to?" asked Mum, following Mrs Foster-Smith out of the room.

"It's Stage Two. It's all to do with dragonpox," Ellen began explaining. "Mirror-Belle said that the cure for chickenpox was just the same. You need bubble bath and toothpaste and hair gel and . . ."

"The child's raving – she's delirious," said Mrs Foster-Smith. "I think we ought to call the doctor."

"I don't think it's that bad," said Mum. "Go and put your pyjamas back on, Ellen, and I'll be with you in a minute. I'll see you at the same time next week then, Mrs Foster-Smith. And as I said, maybe you could try playing the pieces just a *little* more quietly."

Back in the bathroom, Ellen finished untangling herself. She had just got into her pyjamas when Mum came into the room. She looked round in horror at the empty jars and bottles and the froth everywhere.

"What a horrible mess!" she said.

"It wasn't me – not much of it, any-way. It was Mirror-Belle. She came out

18

of the mirror."

"Oh yes, and I suppose she's gone back into it now."

Ellen looked at the mirror. It was covered in toothpasty bubbles.

"I think you're right," she said.

Mum wiped the bubbles off the mirror. Ellen looked into it. The girl she saw there *did* look like Mirror-Belle, but she moved whenever Ellen moved: it was just her own reflection.

Ellen frowned, suddenly unsure about everything. She couldn't just have imagined Mirror-Belle, could she? Her reflection frowned back.

Mum scurried round the room, tut-tutting and clearing up the mess. The worst part was when she discovered how little of her Blue Moon perfume was left.

"I know I leave you on your own a lot when I do my piano-teaching, but I *did* think you were old enough not to do things like this," she said. "You should be in bed with those chickenpox – though I must say, they do look quite a bit better. That big one on your nose seems to have disappeared!"

Then she caught sight of something in the basin and, looking surprised, picked it up.

"Look – here's your left slipper!" she said. "I'm glad it's turned up at last."

Ellen didn't say anything (that would

only annoy Mum again) but she smiled to herself as she put the slipper on, because she knew whose slipper it really was.

Chapter Two

ELLEN'S CASTLE

Ellen and her mother were in one of the changing rooms of a big department store. They were supposed to be buying a dress for Ellen to wear to her grown-up cousin's wedding, but nothing seemed to fit or look right.

"That greeny-blue colour suits you," said Ellen's mum, "but it's too tight. I'll go and see if they've got a bigger size."

Ellen didn't really care *what* dress she wore to the wedding. No one would be looking at her, since she hadn't been asked to be a bridesmaid – something she felt a bit cross about. She practised making her most hideous face at herself in the mirror – the one where her eye-balls rolled up and almost out of sight and her bottom lip jutted over the top one. If she did that at the wedding, people *would* look at her. But of course she'd be too shy to do it when the time came.

This time, though, the face didn't seem

to be working properly. The eyeballs in the mirror rolled back to normal, the mouth went back to its ordinary shape, then opened and said, "You look just like that wicked fairy – the one who pricked my finger."

"Mirror-Belle!" exclaimed Ellen. "What are you doing here?"

Mirror-Belle stepped out of the mirror. She was wearing a too-tight, greeny-blue dress just like the one Ellen had on.

"I see you've moved house," she said, looking around her.

"This isn't a house, it's a shop," said Ellen, but Mirror-Belle wasn't listening. She had picked up Ellen's coat from the floor where it was lying inside out, and was putting it on that way, so that the tartan lining was on the outside.

"Not bad," she said, looking at her reflection. Then, "Come on, let's see what your cook has made for lunch." And she walked out

of the changing room.

"No! Stop!" cried Ellen. "Give me back my coat!" She ran after Mirror-Belle, who was merrily weaving her way around the rails and stands of clothes.

"You *have* got a lot of clothes," she said when Ellen caught up with her. "Almost as many as me, though not such beautiful ones, of course. I don't suppose you've got a ballgown made of rose petals stitched together with spider's thread, have you?"

"No, I haven't," said Ellen. "But I don't think I'd want one. Wouldn't the rose petals shrivel up and die?"

Mirror-Belle thought for a moment and then said, "No, they've been dipped in a magic fountain which keeps them fresh for ever."

By this stage they had reached the escalator. Mirror-Belle hopped on to it.

"This is fun," she said. "Does it go down to the dungeons?"

"No," said Ellen, riding down beside her. "It goes down to the food department."

"The banqueting hall, do you mean?" asked Mirror-Belle. "Oh good, I'm starving."

She skipped off the escalator. They were in the fruit and vegetable section of the food department. Mirror-Belle picked up a potato and put it down again in disgust.

"It's *raw*!" she said. "How does your cook expect us to eat that?" She inspected the cabbages and cauliflowers. "What sort of banquet is *this* supposed to be?" she asked. "None of the food is cooked at all."

"It's not *supposed* to be cooked – people take it home to cook," Ellen tried to explain. "Look, Mirror-Belle, do give me back my raincoat – I must get back to Mum."

"These apples look all right," said Mirror-Belle, picking one up and taking a large bite out of it. She picked up another one and did the same. "With green and red apples like these I only ever bite the green side," she explained. "You can't be too careful – there could be a wicked queen going round putting poison into the red sides. Look what happened to my friend Snow White." She took a bite out of another apple.

Just then a shop assistant came up.

"Stop eating the fruit," she said to Mirror-Belle.

"Start cooking the vegetables!" Mirror-Belle said back to her.

The shop assistant looked startled, and asked Mirror-Belle where her mum or dad was.

"Sitting on their thrones, I expect," said Mirror-Belle. "Come on, Ellen, let's go and play in your bedroom." She grabbed Ellen's hand and pulled her into a lift.

"Does this go up to the battlements?" she asked as the doors closed.

"No," said Ellen. "You seem to think this is some kind of castle but it's not, it's a—"

"Ah, *here's* your bedroom," said Mirror-Belle as the lift doors opened on the second floor. They were in the furniture department. Mirror-Belle darted past some armchairs and sofas to an area full of beds and mattresses. She flung herself

down on a double bed and almost immediately sprang off it again.

"I hope you don't sleep on *that* one,"
she said. "I certainly couldn't
sleep a wink on it."

"No, I don't," said Ellen.
"This isn't my—"

"Good," said Mirror-Belle,
"because there's a pea under the mattress."

"How do you know?"

"We princesses can always tell," said
Mirror-Belle, and she flopped down on to
another bed. "Ugh!" she said. "There's a
baked bean under this one – horribly
lumpy. Lie down and maybe you'll be
able to feel it too."

Ellen giggled. She looked around.
There wasn't a shop assistant in sight.
She lay down on the bed next to Mirror-
Belle. It felt wonderfully springy and
comfortable.

"I can't feel anything," she said.

"That must be because you're not a princess," said Mirror-Belle. "Ordinary people have to bounce to detect peas and beans under mattresses. Like this." She got to her feet and began to jump up and down on the bed.

"Come on!" she said.

Ellen looked around again. There were still no shop assistants to be seen. She joined Mirror-Belle and soon the two of them were bouncing about on the bed,

making the springs of the mattress twang.

"This is nearly as good as the school trampoline," said Ellen breathlessly.

"It's not as good as the *palace* trampoline," said Mirror-Belle. "I once bounced right up into the clouds from that."

"Did you come down all right?"

"No, I didn't," said Mirror-Belle. "The North Wind saw me up there and swept me away to the land of ice."

"What happened then?"

But Ellen never found out because at that moment an angry-looking shop assistant came towards them.

"Quick! Let's run!" Ellen said. But Mirror-Belle had a different idea. She jumped off the bed and advanced towards the assistant as angrily as he was advancing towards them.

"Ah, there you are at last!" she said, before he had a chance to speak. "I want to complain about the state of this bedroom. Peas and beans under all the mattresses – it's disgraceful! Set to work removing them immediately or you'll be fired from the castle!" And with that she linked her arm in Ellen's, turned and strode off towards the escalator. The shop assistant was left gawping as they sailed up to the toy department.

"So this is your playroom, is it?" asked Mirror-Belle.

Ellen tried to explain that they weren't *her* toys, but Mirror-Belle was already emptying the pieces of a jigsaw puzzle out on to the floor.

"Too much sky in this one," she said, and moved on.

"Aren't you going to clear it up?" asked Ellen.

"What, and let your lazy servants get even lazier? Certainly not."

Mirror-Belle continued down the aisle of toys, emptying out various boxes, not

satisfied till she
reached a shelf full
of cuddly toys.
There were teddies
and rabbits, pup-
pies and monkeys,
but Mirror-Belle
picked up a furry
green frog and
kissed it on the nose.

"Why are you doing that?" asked Ellen.

"I'm turning him into a prince," said
Mirror-Belle. "Princesses can do that,
you know."

"Even *furry* frogs?"

"Yes, they just turn into furry princes,
that's all. This one seems to want to stay
a frog, though," said Mirror-Belle. "All
right, you silly creature, away you leap,"
and she threw the frog across the shop
and turned her attention to a teddy.

"I've never tried it on a bear," she said.

But Ellen had noticed a man coming towards them from about where the frog must have landed. He looked even crosser than the bed man had done. She tugged at Mirror-Belle's sleeve in alarm, but Mirror-Belle looked delighted to see the man.

"Don't you see, it's the *prince*," she said. "He doesn't look a very nice prince, mind you," she went on as the man drew closer. "You're not very furry either," as he came right up to them, "unless you count your funny woolly moustache."

"What do you think you're doing?" the man asked.

"Aren't you going to say thank you?" Mirror-Belle said to him.

"What, for throwing toys around?"

"No, for breaking the spell, of course," said Mirror-Belle. "Though if I'd known what a bad-tempered prince you'd turn out to be I wouldn't have bothered. Can't say I blame that witch for turning you into a frog in the first place. Come on, Ellen!"

She turned and walked briskly away, calling over her shoulder, "And if you think you're going to marry me you've got another think coming."

The man stood rooted to the spot for a few moments, too astounded to follow them. By the time he did, Mirror-Belle and Ellen had dived into a lift. Mirror-Belle pressed the top button.

"Perhaps *this*'ll take us to the battlements at last," she said.

"It says 'Offices Only'," said Ellen.

When they got out they were in a corridor with a few doors leading off it. One of the doors was ajar and Ellen could hear a familiar voice coming from it.

"I only went out for a couple of minutes to look for another dress, and when

I got back she'd gone."

Ellen couldn't bear to hear Mum sounding so upset.

"Come with me," she said to Mirror-Belle and ran into the room. Her mother was there with another lady.

"Oh *there* you are, darling," said Mum, hugging her. "Where *have* you been?"

"With Mirror-Belle. She took my coat so I had to follow her," said Ellen. "She's just outside." She took her mother's hand and pulled her into the corridor. There was no one there.

"You didn't mention another little girl," said the shop lady to Mum.

"There isn't one really – it's just my daughter's imaginary friend."

"She's not imaginary, she's real," Ellen protested.

The light outside the lift showed that it was still on the top floor. "She must be in here," said Ellen, pressing the button.

The doors opened. Apart from a crumpled raincoat with a tartan lining lying on the floor, the lift was empty. Where on earth was Princess Mirror-Belle?

It was only then that Ellen noticed something which she should have spotted before.

The walls of the lift were covered in mirrors.

Princess Mirror-Belle had disappeared!

Chapter Three

SNOW WHITE AND THE EIGHT DWARFS

Ellen's big brother Luke was singing again.

"Seven little hats on seven little heads. Seven little pillows on seven little beds," he sang, standing on a ladder and dabbing paint on to the branches of a canvas tree. A blob of paint landed on Ellen's hand. She was squatting on the stage, painting the tree trunk.

Ellen sighed heavily – more because of the song than the blob of paint. Luke had been singing the seven dwarfs' song almost non-stop ever since he'd joined the local drama group and got a part in the Christmas pantomime.

"Seven pairs of trousers on fourteen little legs," he sang now.

"No one could call *your* legs little," said Ellen. "You should be acting a giant, not a dwarf."

"There aren't any giants in *Snow White*, dumbo," said Luke. "Anyway, I told you, we all walk about on our knees."

"So that Sally Hart can pat you on the head," said Ellen. She knew that Luke was keen on Sally Hart. In fact, she guessed that he was only in the pantomime because Sally was acting Snow White.

Luke blushed but all he said was, "Shut up or I won't get you a ticket for tonight."

The first performance of *Snow White* was that evening, and at the last minute the director had decided that the forest needed a couple of extra trees. Luke had volunteered to go and paint them, and Mum had persuaded him to take Ellen along.

Although Ellen was too shy to want to be in the play, it was fun being in the theatre in front of all the rows of empty seats. But Luke wouldn't let her have a go on the ladder, and soon she had painted the bottom of the two tree trunks.

Luke was getting quite carried away with the leaves and acorns, still singing the annoying song all the time. He didn't seem to notice when Ellen wandered off to explore the theatre. She opened a door in a narrow passageway behind the stage.

The room was dark and Ellen switched on the light – or rather, the lights: there was a whole row of bulbs, all shining brightly above a long mirror. This must be one of the dressing rooms.

Some beards were hanging up on a row

of hooks. Ellen guessed they belonged to the seven dwarfs. She unhooked one and tried it on. It was quite tickly.

"Seven little beards on seven little chins," she sang into the mirror.

"And seven mouldy cauliflowers in seven smelly bins," her reflection sang back at her.

But of course it wasn't her reflection. It was Princess Mirror-Belle.

Quickly, Ellen turned her back, hoping that Mirror-Belle would stay in the mirror. Mirror-Belle was the last person she wanted to see just now. Their adventures together always seemed to land Ellen in trouble.

But it was too late. Mirror-Belle had climbed out of the mirror and was tapping Ellen on the shoulder.

"Let's have a look at your beard," she said, and then, as Ellen turned round, "I'd shave it off if I were you – it doesn't suit you."

"It's only a play one," said Ellen. "Anyway, you've got one too."

"I know." Mirror-Belle sighed. "The hairdresser said the wrong spell and I ended up with a beard instead of short hair."

"Couldn't the hairdresser use scissors instead of spells?" asked Ellen.

"Good heavens no," said Mirror-Belle. "An ordinary one could, maybe, but this is the *palace* hairdresser we're talking about."

She turned to a rail of costumes, pulled a robin outfit off its hanger and held it up against herself.

"Put that back!" cried Ellen, and then, "You'll get it all painty!"

They both looked at Mirror-Belle's left hand, which had paint on it, just like Ellen's right one.

"Have you been painting trees too?" Ellen asked.

"No, of course not." Mirror-Belle looked thoughtful as she hung the robin costume back on the rail. Then, "No – trees have been painting *me*," she said.

Ellen couldn't help laughing. "How can they do *that*?" she asked.

"Not *all* trees can do it," replied Mirror-Belle. "Just

the ones in the magic forest. They bend down their branches and dip them into the muddy lake and paint anyone who comes past."

"How strange," said Ellen.

"I don't think it's so strange as people painting trees, which is what you say you've been doing," said Mirror-Belle.

"They're not real trees," Ellen explained. "They're for a play."

Mirror-Belle looked quite interested. "Can I help?" she asked.

"No, you certainly can't," said Ellen, horrified, but Mirror-Belle wasn't put off.

"What sort of trees are they?" she asked. "I'm very good at painting bananas. And pineapples."

"Pineapples don't grow on trees, and anyway—" but Ellen broke off because she heard the stage door bang.

"Ellen! Where are you?" came Luke's voice.

"I'm coming!" Ellen yelled. Then she hissed to Mirror-Belle, "Get back into the mirror! Don't mess about with the costumes! And *stay away from the trees*!"

That evening Ellen was back in the theatre, sitting in the audience next to Mum and Dad. *Snow White* was about to start.

Mum squeezed Ellen's hand. "You look nervous," she said. "Don't worry – I'm sure Luke will be fine."

But it wasn't Luke that Ellen was nervous about – it was Mirror-Belle. What had she been up to in the empty theatre all afternoon? Ellen was terrified that when the curtain went up, the trees would be covered in tropical fruit and the costumes would be covered in paint.

The curtain went up. There were no bananas or pineapples to be seen. The forest looked beautiful. Dad leaned across Mum's seat and whispered, "Very well-painted trees, Ellen."

Sally Hart – or rather, Snow White – looked beautiful too, with her black hair, big eyes and rosy cheeks. Over her arm she carried a basket, and she fed bread-crumbs to a chorus of hungry robins. None of them seemed to have paint on their costumes.

Ellen breathed a sigh of relief.

Everything was all right after all! Mirror-Belle must have gone back into the dressing-room mirror.

A palace scene came next. When the wicked Queen looked into her magic mirror and asked,

"Mirror, mirror on the wall,

Who is the fairest one of all?"

for an awful moment Ellen was afraid that Mirror-Belle might come leaping out of the mirror, shouting "I am!" But of course she could only do that if it was *Ellen* looking into the mirror. Stop being so jumpy, Ellen told herself – Mirror-Belle is safely back in her own world.

When the scene changed to the dwarfs' cottage, Mum gave Ellen a nudge. Soon Luke would be coming on stage!

And yes, now Snow White was asleep in one of the beds, and here came the dwarfs, shuffling in through the cottage door. Ellen knew that they were walking on their knees but the costumes were so good, with shoes stitched on to the front of the baggy trousers, that you couldn't really tell.

Luke was acting the bossiest dwarf – typical, Ellen thought. He told the others to hang up their jackets and set the table. Then they started to dance around and sing the song that Ellen was so tired of hearing.

"Seven little jackets on seven little pegs. Seven little eggcups, and seven little eggs."

But something was wrong. One of the dwarfs was singing much louder than the others, and not getting all the words right. When the other dwarfs stopped singing and started to tap out the tune on the table, the dwarf with the loud voice carried on:

"Seven stupid people who don't know how to count. Can't they see that seven

is not the right amount?"

The audience laughed as they realised that there were *eight* dwarfs and not seven. But Ellen didn't laugh. Dwarf number eight had to be Mirror-Belle, and there was bound to be serious trouble ahead.

Up on the stage, Luke looked furious. He stopped tapping the table and started chasing Mirror-Belle round the room. He was trying to chase her out of the door but she kept dodging him as she carried on singing:

"Eight little spoons and eight little bowls. Sixteen little woolly socks with sixteen great big holes."

Ellen felt like shouting, or throwing

something, or rushing on to the stage herself and dragging Mirror-Belle off. But that would just make things worse. All she could do was to watch in horror.

In the end, Luke gave up the chase. With one last glare at Mirror-Belle he strode over to the bed where Snow White was sleeping. His cross expression changed to one of adoration when Snow White woke up and sang a song.

"Will you stay with us?" Luke begged her when the song had finished.

"Yes, do stay and look after us," said another dwarf.

"We need someone to comb our beards."

"And wash our clothes."

"And shine our shoes."

"And cook our meals."

"And clean our house."

All the dwarfs except Mirror-Belle were chiming in.

"There's nothing I'd like better!" exclaimed Snow White.

Mirror-Belle turned on her. "You must be joking," she said angrily. "You shouldn't be doing things like that – you're a *princess*! You should be bossing *them* about, not the other way round."

The audience laughed – except for Ellen – and Snow White's mouth fell open. Ellen felt sorry for her: she obviously didn't know what to say. But Luke came to the rescue.

"Be quiet!" he ordered Mirror-Belle.

"You don't know anything about princesses."

"Of course I do – I *am* one!" Mirror-Belle retorted. "I'm just in disguise as a dwarf. I thought Snow White might need some protection against that horrible Queen. I'm pretty sure she's going to be along soon with a tray of poisoned apples, and—"

"Shut up, you're spoiling the story!" hissed Luke, and put a hand over Mirror-Belle's mouth. Snow White looked at him in admiration. Luke made a sign to someone offstage, and a second later the curtain came down. It was the end of the first half.

"Isn't Luke good?" said Mum in the interval. "He never told us he had such a big part."

"That little girl playing the extra dwarf is a hoot, isn't she?" said Dad.

"She sounds a bit like you, Ellen. Who is she?"

"I don't know," muttered Ellen. It was no use mentioning Mirror-Belle to her parents, who just thought she was an imaginary friend. Ellen licked her ice cream but she was too worried to enjoy it properly. What would Mirror-Belle get up to in the second half of the show?

The curtain went up again. Snow White was sweeping the dwarfs' cottage. Ellen was relieved that there was no sign of Mirror-Belle. She must have gone off to work with the other dwarfs.

The wicked Queen appeared at the cottage window. She looked quite different – like an old woman – as she held out a tray of apples and offered one to Snow White.

"The dwarfs made me promise not to buy anything from a stranger," said Snow White.

"There's no need to buy," replied the disguised Queen. "Just open the window, and I'll give you one!"

Snow White opened the window and took an apple in her hand. She still looked doubtful.

"Don't you trust me?" asked the Queen. "Look, I'll take a bite out of it myself first to prove that it's all right." She did this and handed the apple back to Snow White.

Snow White had just opened her mouth when a voice cried, "Stop!" and a second figure appeared at the cottage window. Oh no! It was Mirror-Belle.

"Stop! Don't you realise, she took that bite out of the green half of the apple. It's the red half that's poisoned!" she warned Snow White.

Snow White took no notice and was about to bite into the apple when

Mirror-Belle snatched it from her. She snatched the tray of apples from the Queen too. The next moment she had burst in through the cottage door, pursued by the Queen.

Some steps led down from the stage into the audience, and Mirror-Belle ran down them. She ran through the audience, the Queen hot on her heels.

When Mirror-Belle reached Ellen's

seat she whispered, "Here, take this!" and thrust the tray of apples on to Ellen's lap. Ellen didn't know what to do, but was saved from doing anything by the Queen, who snatched the tray back. Mirror-Belle grabbed it from her again and ran on.

Meanwhile, Snow White, who had run off the back of the stage, reappeared holding Luke's hand and followed by the other dwarfs. They joined in the chase, round and round the audience and back on to the stage. Luke overtook the others. He caught Mirror-Belle by the shoulders and shook her.

"Give back those apples!" he ordered.

"What! Do you *want* Snow White to be poisoned?" protested Mirror-Belle. "Some friend you are!"

"Who is she, anyway?" asked Snow White – except that she didn't sound like Snow White any more, she sounded like

Sally Hart.

"I don't know but we'll soon find out!" said Luke – sounding like Luke and not a dwarf – and he ripped Mirror-Belle's beard off.

"Ellen, it's you!" he exclaimed.

"Oh no I'm not!" said Mirror-Belle. "Your sister Ellen is in the audience – there, look!" She pointed, and to Ellen's embarrassment not only Luke but everyone else on the stage and in the audience was looking at her.

Not for long, though. Soon all eyes were back on Mirror-Belle, who was throwing apples into the audience.

"Don't eat them, *and don't give them back*!" she ordered.

Just then a man in a suit came on to the stage. Ellen recognised him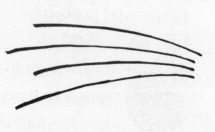

as Mr Turnbull, the director. He strode up to Mirror-Belle.

"I don't know who you are or where you come from, but you'd better go back there before I call the police!" he said.

"Don't worry, I will!" said Mirror-Belle. Mr Turnbull made a grab for her but she dodged him and ran out through the cottage door. Mr Turnbull and all the actors followed her, and Ellen heard the Queen shout, "Oh no! She's got my mirror now!"

A moment later, Mirror-Belle was climbing back into the cottage through the open window, clutching the Queen's mirror. She scuttled into the dwarfs' cupboard just as everyone else came charging back in through the door.

 "Where is she?" asked Mr Turnbull, with his back to the cupboard. Mirror-Belle popped her head out.

"She's behind you!" yelled the audience. Mr Turnbull turned round but now the cupboard door was shut.

"Oh no she's not!" said Mr Turnbull.

"OH YES SHE IS!" the audience shouted back.

Snow White opened the cupboard door and peered in.

"Is she there?" asked Mr Turnbull.

"I don't think so," said Snow White. She picked up her broom and swept around inside, just to make sure. "What's this?" she asked, as she swept an object out of the cupboard.

"It's my magic mirror!" said the Queen. "So she must have been here."

"Well, she's gone now, thank goodness," said Mr Turnbull. He turned to face the audience.

"I'm sorry about all this, ladies and gentlemen," he said. "Anyone who wants their money back can ask at the box

_ 60 _*

office. But now, on with the show!"

"Seven little cups and seven little plates," sang Mum next day, as she served up Ellen's lunch. Luke was having a lie-in.

"Oh, Mum, don't *you* start!"

"Sorry. Wasn't Luke brilliant last night? I can't wait to show him the piece in the paper."

"Let's have a look."

Mum passed Ellen the paper, and this is what she read:

"The Pinkerton Players' performance of *Snow White* last night was a comic triumph. The hilarious chase scene was hugely enjoyable, and so was the entertaining scene in which the director pretended to offer the audience their money back.

"All the cast gave excellent performances, especially Sally Hart as Snow White and Luke Page as the bossy dwarf, but the real star of the show was the child who played the Eighth Dwarf. Sadly, she was not present at the curtain call. Perhaps she was too young to stay up so late.

"I have only one criticism of the show. Why did this child star's name not appear in the programme? Everyone wants to know who she is, and everyone wants to see more of her."

Yes, thought Ellen. Everyone except me.

Chapter Four

PARTY HOPPERS

"Happy birthday, Anthony," said Ellen, holding out a present. Her six-year-old cousin snatched it and ripped off the paper.

"It's a book! I hate books – they're boring," he said, throwing it on the floor. "Why couldn't you get me a video?"

Anthony was a pain, and the most painful thing about him was that he was exactly two years younger than Ellen's friend Livvy. Their parties were on the same day, and Mum always insisted that Ellen went to Anthony's one. It just wasn't fair – especially this year, when

Livvy's eighth birthday party was in the swimming pool, with inflatables to bounce about on and pizzas in the café afterwards.

"Let's play a few games before tea," said Anthony's mother, Auntie Pam, brightly. Ellen's heart sank even lower. The games were always the same – Stick the Tail on the Donkey, Pass the Parcel and Musical Chairs, and Anthony always won at least two of them – his mother saw to that.

Auntie Pam stuck up a big picture of a donkey without a tail and gave each child a paper tail with their name written on it.

"How about you going first, as you're the oldest, Ellen?" she suggested. She tied a scarf round Ellen's eyes and guided her towards the donkey picture. Ellen pinned the tail on to it blindly and everyone laughed. Auntie Pam removed

the scarf and Ellen saw that the tail was
sticking on to one of the donkey's ears.

All the other guests had goes, till the
donkey had tails growing out of its legs,
mane and nose. Then it was Anthony's
turn. "Don't tie it too tight!" he ordered
his mother. When he was standing in
front of the donkey picture Ellen noticed
him tilting his head back and she
guessed that he was peeping out from
below the scarf. Sure enough, he stuck
the tail on to exactly the right spot.

"Brilliant, birthday boy!" said Auntie
Pam, and presented him with the prize,
which was an enormous box of chocolates.

"Now let's play Dead Lions," she said. This was a game where you all had to lie on the floor and try not to move. If you moved you were Out – unless you were Anthony, in which case you squealed, "I didn't move, I didn't move, I *didn't*!" until your mother gave you another chance.

Auntie Pam produced a box of face paints and suggested that for a change the children might like to be different jungle animals – not just lions. She got Ellen to help her paint zebra and tiger stripes on to the younger children's faces, in front of the big mirror in the hall.

The made-up children raced back into the sitting room and Ellen was left to paint her own face. She felt in rather a poisonous mood so she decided to be a snake. She picked up the green stick and was about to start painting her face when she saw the mirror lips move and heard a familiar voice.

"Are you sure you've been invited?" asked Mirror-Belle.

Ellen felt ridiculously glad to see her. It was true that Mirror-Belle usually spelled trouble, but she was much more fun than Anthony and his friends.

"Of course I've been invited. It's my cousin's party," Ellen replied, glancing around to check that no one else could

see Mirror-Belle climbing out of the mirror.

Mirror-Belle looked around too. "Oh dear," she said. "I seem to be in the wrong place. I'm supposed to be at the wood nymphs' party. That was why I was painting my face green." Like Ellen, she had a box of face paints in one hand and a green stick in the other.

"I see you're planning to go green too," she said. "Is your cousin a wood elf or something?"

"No, he's a monster," said Ellen, and she told Mirror-Belle about Anthony and about how she really wanted to go to Livvy's swimming party.

"And so you shall!" said Mirror-Belle, sounding like the Fairy Godmother in *Cinderella*. "Off you go! I'll stay here and pretend to be you."

Ellen felt torn. "But Mirror-Belle . . . I don't know . . . could you really do that?"

"Of course," replied Mirror-Belle. "I'm an expert at pretending. In fact, I've got several gold medals for it."

Ellen could well believe that; she often wondered how many of Mirror-Belle's stories about herself were true. All the same, she was still worried about leaving her at Anthony's party.

"But you'd have to *behave* like me, not like you," she said. "You'd have to be shy and sensible, and you'd have to promise not to—" but she never finished the sentence because she heard Auntie Pam calling her.

"Coming!" said Mirror-Belle, and strode into the sitting room. There was no choice left. Ellen crept to the front door and let herself out.

The swimming pool wasn't far from Anthony's house. Ellen ran all the way. Livvy and the other guests had only just arrived, and Livvy's mother was giving them all 20p pieces for the lockers.

"Ellen!" shouted Livvy. "That's brilliant – I thought you had to go to your cousin's party. Where are your swimming things?"

"Oh dear. I left them at home," said Ellen. She felt foolish, particularly as she was still clutching the box of face paints.

"Shall I phone your mother and ask her to bring them round?" offered Livvy's mother.

"Er . . . no, she's gone out," said Ellen.

"Well, never mind – I expect you can borrow a costume and towel from Lost Property," and Livvy's mother went off to organise this.

"Is that my present? I love face paints!" said Livvy.

"Er, yes," said Ellen, thrusting the box into her hands. "I'm sorry I didn't have time to wrap them up." She'd never told Livvy about Mirror-Belle and this didn't seem a good time to start.

The Lost Property costume was a bit loose but Ellen didn't

mind. It was wonderful to be in the water with Livvy and the others. They had the pool all to themselves. There was a huge inflatable sea monster, and a pirate ship and a desert island. Livvy made up a really good game called Sharks, where you had to swim from the desert island to the ship without being caught by a shark. If you got caught you were taken to the sea monster and had to wait on its back to be rescued. Ellen was a fast swimmer and managed to rescue several fishes from the sharks. That was fun, but the best thing about the game was that Anthony wasn't there to cheat and squeal and clamour for a prize. (There weren't any prizes, which was another good thing.)

Ellen was in the middle of a particularly daring rescue when Livvy, who was one of the sharks, grabbed her by the shoulder strap of her costume. Ellen

tried to swim away and the strap snapped.

The swimming-pool attendant beckoned to Ellen. "Pop into the changing area and they'll find you a safety pin," she said.

As Ellen fixed the strap in front of the mirror in the changing area she remembered Mirror-Belle and wondered how she was getting on at Anthony's party.

She didn't have to wonder for very long.

"Be careful with that pin," said Mirror-Belle. "You don't want to prick your finger and end up asleep for a hundred years."

At that moment Ellen felt she would like nothing better. How *could* Mirror-Belle do this to her?

"Mirror-Belle, stay there! Don't come out of the mirror! You're not supposed to be here! Go back to Anthony's party!"

"No thank you very much." Mirror-Belle jumped down beside Ellen. She too held a safety pin and wore a baggy swimming costume with a broken shoulder strap. "I couldn't stand another game of Musical Thrones," she said.

"Don't you mean Musical Chairs?" asked Ellen.

"Yes, I think that *is* what they called it," said Mirror-Belle. "Musical Thrones is much better. You leap from throne to throne, and the thrones play tunes when you land on them."

"I hope you didn't leap about on the chairs?" said Ellen.

"I did try, but it was a bit hard because Tantrummy's mother kept taking them away."

"Anthony, not Tantrummy," Ellen corrected her, though Tantrummy did seem a better name for him. "Anyway, of course his mum took the chairs away – that's the whole point of Musical Chairs: you take a chair away every time the music stops."

"Well, all that furniture-shifting seemed a lot of hard work for Tantrummy's mother," said Mirror-Belle. "She obviously needed some servants to help her. I can't think why she got so angry when I telephoned that removal firm."

Ellen gasped. "They didn't come, did they?"

"No – Tantrummy's mother cancelled

them and made us play Keep the Parcel instead."

"Pass the Parcel, you mean."

"I can't remember exactly what they called it," said Mirror-Belle, "but it took me absolutely ages to unwrap the parcel – it was a terrible waste of so much wrapping paper – and in the end there was only a tiny bag of sweets in the middle."

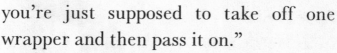

"But you're not supposed to unwrap the whole thing – you're just supposed to take off one wrapper and then pass it on."

"Don't be ridiculous, Ellen," said Mirror-Belle. "Didn't you know it's very rude to give away something which has been given to you?"

"I don't suppose Anthony was very

pleased when you unwrapped the whole thing yourself."

"No, he started up a game of his own called Scream the House Down," said Mirror-Belle.

Ellen almost laughed, but then she remembered that she was the one who would be accused of all the things Mirror-Belle had done.

"I hope Auntie Pam didn't kick you out," she said.

"No – she summoned her magician," said Mirror-Belle.

"Oh, was there a conjuror? Was he good?"

"Unfortunately not. He just did a lot of tricks – not real magic at all. In the end I had to lend him a hand."

"How do you mean?"

"He offered to make one of us disappear," said Mirror-Belle. "He had a big long box and he asked Anthony to climb into it. Then he spun the box round a few times and opened a flap. We all looked into the box and it *did* look as though Anthony had disappeared. But then I lifted a different flap and there he was!"

"That was a bit mean to spoil the trick," said Ellen.

"Wait – I haven't finished," said Mirror-Belle. "I spotted that there was a mirror inside the empty part of the box – it made that space look bigger, which was why it looked as though Anthony had disappeared."

"I'm not sure if I understand," said Ellen.

"Never mind – I'm sure you'll understand the next bit," Mirror-Belle told her. "I climbed into the part of the box with the mirror in it and told the magician to close the lid, and then . . ."

"You disappeared through the mirror!" finished Ellen.

"Precisely. The magician must be delighted. At last it looks as if he's done some real magic!"

"I shouldn't think he's delighted at *all*! He's probably horrified," said Ellen, feeling horrified herself. "They must all be looking for me! I'll have to go back there – or else you will." Oh dear, which would be worse? To send Mirror-Belle back to Anthony's or to leave her in the swimming pool?

Just then Ellen heard voices. Livvy and the others were coming to get changed. Ellen ran and opened her locker, scooped out her clothes and dived into a changing cubicle. As she closed the door she heard Livvy greet Mirror-Belle:

"What took you so long, Ellen? It's time for the pizzas now. I'm going to have ham and pineapple."

"I'll have dragon and tomato," said Mirror-Belle, and Livvy laughed.

Ellen changed quickly, and rubbed her hair as dry as she could. When she reckoned that all the others were in the cubicles she made her getaway. As she left the changing area she heard Livvy asking, "What's happened to your clothes, Ellen?" and Mirror-Belle replying, "I must have left them in the palace."

Instead of ringing Anthony's bell, Ellen crept round to the back door. It was unlocked and she tiptoed inside. She could hear voices calling her name upstairs; they must be searching the bedrooms. She peeped round the door of the sitting room. To her amazement the room was empty. On the floor was the long box which Mirror-Belle must have been talking about. Ellen lifted the lid and squeezed in. It was dark and cramped inside.

Almost immediately she heard the doorbell, followed by footsteps and voices in the hall.

"What do you mean, 'Just disappeared'?" This was her mother's voice.

"It's magic!" This was one of the children. "He's a really good conjuror. I want him to come to my party."

Then the conjuror: "It was nothing to do with me! I didn't even ask the wretched child to get into the box!"

"I want to see this box!" Mum's voice sounded really near now and Ellen realised that everyone had come into the sitting room.

"She's not there. We've looked hundreds of times," said Auntie Pam.

The next second the lid was opened and light streamed in.

"Ellen!" said Mum. Ellen climbed out and hugged her. Everyone clustered round.

"Fancy keeping her stuck in there all

that time!" Mum accused the conjuror. "And why is her hair all damp?"

"I can't understand it!" he said. "This has never happened before."

Ellen felt sorry for him. She decided to tell the truth. "It's not his fault," she said. "It was Mirror-Belle."

"Who's Mirror-Belle?" asked one of the children.

"It's Ellen's imaginary friend," explained Mum.

"What an imagination she's got!" said Auntie Pam. "She was making up all sorts of extraordinary stories earlier on." But Mum didn't hear this, because Anthony had started to clamour, "Why didn't *I* disappear? *I* want to be invisible! It's not fair – I want another go!"

When Ellen and Mum got home, Luke was on the phone.

"It's all right, here she is," Ellen heard

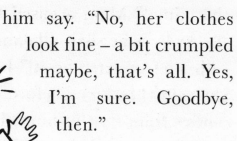

him say. "No, her clothes look fine – a bit crumpled maybe, that's all. Yes, I'm sure. Goodbye, then."

"Who was that?" asked Mum.

"This weird woman," said Luke. "Mrs Duck or someone."

"Was it Livvy Drake's mother?"

"Yes, Drake, that was it. She wanted to know if Ellen was all right."

"Why shouldn't she be all right?" asked Mum.

"Don't ask me. I couldn't understand what the woman was on about. Something about Ellen's clothes getting stolen from the swimming pool."

"But Ellen wasn't at the swimming pool."

"That's what I told her, but she kept on about it. She said Ellen's locker was empty and there must have been a thief. She said they had to get some different clothes from Lost Property."

"She's obviously mixing Ellen up with some other child," said Mum.

"And then she said Ellen just disappeared when the rest of them were eating pizzas," went on Luke. "She was worried she might have been kidnapped."

"How strange," said Mum. She gave Ellen another hug. "I think you've had quite enough adventures for one day without being kidnapped, don't you?" she asked.

"Yes," said Ellen. "I certainly do."

Chapter Five

WOBBLESDAY

Ellen hadn't seen Mirror-Belle for a few weeks. At the beginning of the summer holidays her family had moved house. The new house was in a different town, and Ellen had the feeling that Mirror-Belle had lost track of her. If so, she wasn't exactly sorry. Their adventures always seemed to end up with Ellen getting into trouble and Mirror-Belle escaping. Still, just sometimes Ellen found herself looking in the mirror and half-hoping that her reflection would do something surprising. She would have liked someone to play with. There weren't any children in either of the houses next door. A girl of about her own age lived further down the street, but Ellen was too shy to say hello. She hoped she would make some friends when she started at her new school, but she felt quite nervous about that too.

When a fair came to the common near their new house, Mum said Ellen's big brother Luke could take her as long as he stayed with her. This sounded like fun, but the trouble was that Ellen and Luke wanted to do different things. Luke liked the kind of rides where you went flying and plunging about, preferably upside down and back to front. Ellen liked being scared too, but not in an upside-down sort of way. She wanted to go on the ghost train, but Luke said that was just for kids.

"I'll see you back here in an hour, OK?" said Luke. They were in the Wobbly

Mirror Hall.

Ellen pretended to forget that Luke was supposed to stay with her.

"All right," she said. She wasn't looking at Luke but at herself in one of the wobbly mirrors. Her mouth was gaping like a cave in her droopy chin, above a long wiggly body and little waddly legs. "Look at me!" she said, laughing and pointing, but Luke had already gone. Instead, it was the peculiar reflection who replied.

"Don't point, it's rude," she said, and stepped out of the mirror.

"Mirror-Belle, it's you!" said Ellen, and laughed again. "You've gone all funny and wobbly."

"Of course I'm wobbly, it's Wobblesday today, isn't it?"

"No, it's Wednesday," said Ellen.

"Call it that if you like," said Mirror-Belle, waddling out of the Mirror Hall on her short legs, "but where *I* come from it's a Wobblesday, and everyone wobbles on Wobblesdays. It's a rule my father the King made. Even the *palace* goes wobbly on Wobblesdays. A bit like that one," she added, pointing to a bouncy castle on which some children were jumping about. The finger Mirror-Belle was pointing with looked like a wiggly knitting needle and Ellen laughed again. She found she was really glad to see Mirror-Belle after all. She hadn't exactly been looking forward to going on the ghost train by herself.

"Have you got any money?" Ellen asked. Mirror-Belle had three 50p and two 20p pieces.

"Exactly the same as me," said Ellen. "But all the writing is back to front on your coins."

"It's *yours* that are the wrong way round, silly," said Mirror-Belle.

They each gave 50p to the man in charge of the ghost train, who was chewing gum and staring at nothing. He didn't seem to notice Mirror-Belle's strange appearance or the backwards writing.

They got into a carriage of the ghost train behind a woman and a little boy.

"It'll be fun travelling on an ordinary train," said Mirror-Belle. "I've only ever been on a royal one before."

"This one isn't exactly *ordinary*—" Ellen warned, but was interrupted by an eerie voice:

"This is your Guaaaaaard speaking," the voice moaned. "Ride if you dare but prepare for a scare."

"What a silly guard!" said Mirror-Belle. "Why doesn't he tell us what stations we'll be going to and whether we can get tea and snacks on the train?"

The train set off. Almost immediately it plunged into a tunnel. As they turned a corner a luminous monster popped out at them. A little girl in front screamed.

"This is disgraceful, frightening inno-cent children!" said Mirror-Belle. As she spoke, a huge spider dangled down from the ceiling and the girl screamed again.

"Don't they ever sweep their tunnels?" said Mirror-Belle.

She reached up and grabbed the spider with her long wiggly fingers.

"Go and build your web somewhere else," she said, throwing it over her shoulder. The people in the seats behind screamed.

The train turned another corner, where a ghost loomed out of the darkness and went "Whooo!" at the little girl. She

clutched her mother.

"This is too bad," said Mirror-Belle. She leaned out of the carriage and went "Whooo!" back at the ghost, only much louder. The little girl turned round, saw Mirror-Belle and screamed again. Ellen wasn't surprised: with her gaping mouth and dangling chin Mirror-Belle probably looked like another ghost or monster to the little girl.

A few skeletons, vampires and coffins later the train stopped, and the little girl stopped screaming. "Can we have another go?" she said to her mother.

Mirror-Belle looked around her in disgust. "This is ridiculous," she said. "We haven't gone anywhere at all – we're back where we started. I'm going to complain to the stationmaster." She got out and headed towards the gum-chewing man, but Ellen managed to stop her.

"Why don't we have a go at the hoop-la?" she said. "Look, we could win one of those giant teddies."

Ellen had never won a prize at hoopla. She could never manage to throw her hoop over a peg so that it landed flat, and this time was no different. But for Mirror-Belle it was easy. She just reached out one of her amazingly long arms and put the hoop over the peg. Soon she had won three teddies and a goldfish in a bowl. A little crowd had gathered around them.

"Here, you take these," said Mirror-Belle, thrusting the teddies and goldfish at Ellen and moving on to the coconut shy. The crowd followed.

The man at the coconut shy looked

pleased to see so many people. Ellen missed with her three balls but Mirror-Belle's long arm reached almost to the stands holding the coconuts and she knocked them out with no trouble. The crowd grew bigger and some of the people

 started having goes. The coconut man didn't seem to mind Mirror-Belle winning so often, and even gave her a sack to put the teddies and coconuts in.

"I think you'd better stop before it gets too heavy to carry," said Ellen. "Do you like candyfloss?"

"Wobbably," said Mirror-Belle.

"Don't you mean, 'probably'?"

"No, I mean *wobbably*. That means that if the candyfloss is wobbly I'll like it. You seem to have forgotten that this is Wobblesday. On Wobblesdays we only eat wobbly food."

It took some time to reach the candy-floss stall, as Mirror-Belle could only take tiny steps with her short legs, while her long body wobbled about all over the place.

Mirror-Belle asked for two wobbly candyflosses. The candyfloss seller gave her a funny look but she wiggled the sticks about a lot as she spun the pink stuff round them, and Mirror-Belle decided that would do. Her mouth was so huge that she ate hers in one mouthful and asked for five more.

"I've got yards and yards of tummy to fill, you see," she said, after she'd eaten all five at once.

By now all their money was used up, and Ellen remembered she was supposed to be meeting Luke at the Mirror Hall. They went back there.

Outside the Mirror Hall there was a

sign saying, "Wobbly Mirror-Hall, 20p."

"*Really!*" said Mirror-Belle. "As if it's not bad enough everything being in backwards writing, they can't even spell my name."

She took a felt-tip pen out of her pocket, changed two of the letters and added one. The sign now said, "Wobbly Mirror-Belle, 20p".

"Now, Ellen," she said, "you collect the

money. Remember, it's twenty pence a wobble." She took up a position beside the notice, standing completely still, as if she was playing Musical Statues.

Ellen shuffled from foot to foot, not sure what to do. A few people gathered round.

"Twenty pence for what?" asked one.

"To see her wobble," said Ellen.

"She can't wobble, she's just a statue," said another.

"Isn't she that funny girl that was winning all the coconuts?" asked someone else.

In the end a man handed Ellen 20p, saying he wanted it back if he wasn't satisfied. As Ellen's palm closed round the coin, Mirror-Belle's body began to ripple, like a snake-charmer's snake rearing out of its basket and writhing about. She kept it up for half a minute and then stopped abruptly.

Immediately someone else gave Ellen 20p, and this time Mirror-Belle stretched out one of her long snaky arms. The crowd watched it wobble, curving and bending and eventually tying itself into a knot. Everyone clapped, except for one man who muttered, "It's all done with mirrors," in a knowing way.

The third time, Mirror-Belle wobbled her ears. They bounced up and down like yo-yos, nearly hitting the ground and then springing back up again. By this

time the crowd was quite big, and everybody seemed to be reaching into their pockets.

Then Ellen noticed Luke strolling towards them from a ride called Jaws of Terror, his gelled hair glinting in the sunshine.

"Here comes my brother!" she said to Mirror-Belle.

With one last bounce of her ears Mirror-Belle turned and waddled, surprisingly quickly, into the Mirror Hall.

"Hey, you haven't paid!" the attendant called out.

"I'll pay for her," said Ellen. She gave the attendant two of the three 20ps they had earned, and followed Mirror-Belle, but she was overtaken by several of the crowd, eager for more wobbly stunts. Ellen looked around for Mirror-Belle but couldn't find her. Instead, she bumped into Luke.

"There you are!" he said. "You don't know what you've missed! That Space-Lurcher – it's amazing the way it stops and changes direction just when you're upside down at the top. You really feel you're going to fall out." Then he noticed the goldfish bowl and the sack. He looked inside the sack and saw the teddies and coconuts.

"Did you win all those?" he asked. Ellen could tell he was trying not to sound too impressed. She nearly said, "No, Mirror-Belle did," but she knew Luke wouldn't believe her. She guessed, too, that Mirror-Belle would by now have made her getaway into one of the wobbly mirrors. So instead she answered, "Yes – and I've still got twenty pence left!"

Chapter Six

LOVE-POTION CRISPS

It was the first day of term and Ellen was starting at her new school. Mum took her to the head teacher's office, and the head teacher took her to her classroom.

"This is Ellen, who is going to be joining your class," she announced. All the other children stared at Ellen. She clutched her lunch box tightly and tried to smile.

"Hello, Ellen," said the teacher brightly. "Perhaps you'd like to hang your blazer up in the cloakroom next door? You'll find a peg in there with your name on it."

Ellen found her peg and hung up her blazer. Underneath it she wore a tunic and blouse, and a tie with diagonal green and yellow stripes. Her old school didn't have a uniform, so she had never worn a tie before. She checked in the cloakroom mirror to make sure it was straight.

Yes, the tie looked fine but, oh dear, Ellen didn't feel like going back into the classroom and being stared at again.

She was just turning away from the mirror when a voice said, "You *do* look

worried. Never fear, I'll be there."

Ellen turned back in time to see Mirror-Belle stepping cheerfully out of the mirror. She carried a lunch box just like Ellen's and was wearing the same uniform, except that the stripes in her tie sloped in the opposite direction.

"Mirror-Belle! *You* can't come to school with me!" said Ellen.

"What do you mean, I can't? I just have, haven't I?" said Mirror-Belle. She skipped past Ellen out of the cloakroom and opened the classroom door.

"Hello again, Ellen," said the teacher, and then looked surprised as she saw the real Ellen behind Mirror-Belle.

"I didn't know you had a twin," she said.

"Well, never mind," said Mirror-Belle. "You can't know everything. I don't suppose you know how many fairy godmothers I've got either."

"Now, Ellen, don't be cheeky," said the teacher.

"That's something else you don't know," said Mirror-Belle. "I'm not Ellen, I'm Mirror-Belle."

"Very well, Mirror-Belle, now come and sit down at this table. You and Ellen can be in Orange group."

"I'd rather be in Gold group or Silver group," said Mirror-Belle.

"We don't have either of those, I'm afraid," said the teacher firmly, "but I'm sure you'll get on fine in Orange group if you behave yourself."

She gave out some exercise books and asked the children to write about what they had done in the holidays. Ellen wrote about moving house.

The teacher wandered round the classroom. She came over to Orange group's table and looked over Mirror-Belle's shoulder.

"Yours is a bit difficult to read, Mirror-Belle," she said. "Your letters seem to be the wrong way round. It is easy to get muddled up, I know, especially between 'b's and 'd's."

"Oh, poor you," said Mirror-Belle. "Do you really get as muddled up as all that? Don't worry – I'm sure you'll learn. Perhaps you'd better use a mirror to read my writing."

"That's quite a good idea," said the teacher, and took a mirror out of her handbag. "Yes, I can read it fine now. Mirror-Belle's written a very interesting story," she told the class. "Do you mind if I read it out, Mirror-Belle?"

"Not at all," said Mirror-Belle. "I expect you could do with a bit of reading practice."

The teacher read out Mirror-Belle's story. It went like this:

"I didn't do very much in the holidays because I got turned into a golden statue. You see, my father the King was nice to an old man and so he was given the power to turn everything he touched to gold. By mistake he touched me. In the end I got turned back by being washed in a magic river."

The children all laughed at this story, and the teacher said, "That was good, Mirror-Belle, although I seem to have heard that story before somewhere. What I asked you to write about was what you *really* did in the holidays."

"But I told you, I didn't *do* anything," said Mirror-Belle. "You *can't* when you're a golden statue – you can't move, or eat or brush your hair or anything. I had this awful tickle on my leg and I couldn't even scratch it."

At this point the bell for morning play rang. A friendly girl called Katy took Ellen and Mirror-Belle into the playground where they joined in a game of tig. But two big boys kept bumping into Ellen. They pretended it was by accident but Ellen could tell it was on purpose.

"That's Bruce Baxter and Stephen Hodge," said Katy. "They're *always* like that." Mirror-Belle said nothing but looked very thoughtful.

After playtime the teacher gave out some maths books and asked the children to turn to a page which had a picture of a fruit shop.

"Now," she said, "if one apple costs ten pence and Susan gives the fruit-seller fifty pence, how much change will she get?"

"Hold on a second," said Mirror-Belle. "Look at those apples. Would you say they're half red and half green?"

"What about it, Mirror-Belle?"

"I think Susan ought to watch out," said Mirror-Belle. "How does she know the apple-selling lady hasn't poisoned the apples? She's probably a wicked queen in disguise, trying to get rid of anyone more beautiful than her."

"*Mirror-Belle!*" said the teacher angrily. "I'm not asking you to tell fairy stories. I asked how much *change* Susan would get from her fifty pence. How much do you think?"

"None," said Mirror-Belle. "If that queen's as wicked as I think she is, she'll run off with the fifty pence."

By the time the bell rang for lunch the teacher was looking quite exhausted.

In the dinner hall Ellen and Mirror-Belle sat with Katy and the other children who had brought packed lunches. Unfortunately, these included Bruce Baxter and Stephen Hodge. When the dinner lady wasn't looking Bruce grabbed Ellen's bag of crisps. Then Stephen took Katy's chocolate bar and Bruce snatched another child's yogurt.

They put all the things in a bag along with some other goodies they had stolen.

"They always do that," said Katy. "Then they eat them in the playground."

"But why don't you tell the dinner lady?" asked Ellen.

"If you do that they lie in wait on the way home from school and pounce on you."

Once again Mirror-Belle was being unusually quiet and thoughtful. She had managed to avoid having her lunch stolen, and she took an unopened packet of crisps out into the playground. They looked just like Ellen's crisps except for the writing being back to front.

Katy and her friends had a long skipping rope and they asked Ellen and Mirror-Belle to play with them. But Bruce Baxter and Stephen Hodge kept barging into the game and treading on the rope. Stephen was swinging the bag of stolen food. Just as they were inter-rupting the game for the fourth time, Mirror-Belle said loudly, "I see I've got love-potion-flavoured crisps today."

"What are they?" said Ellen.

"They make you fall in love with the first person you see."

She popped one into her mouth, fixing her eyes on Bruce Baxter.

"Oh, my hero!" she suddenly exclaimed. Then she ran up to him and hugged him. Bruce went red. All the girls laughed at him and so did Stephen.

"Let me shower you with kisses!" said Mirror-Belle, aiming a kiss at Bruce's nose. He turned away and the kiss landed on his ear.

"You were so wonderful when you were spoiling the skipping game," she said. "*Please* do it again and I'll give you *ten* kisses!"

"Leave me alone," said Bruce.

"Never!" cried Mirror-Belle. She bit into another crisp, at the same time staring at Stephen Hodge. "Oh, my darling!" she said. "My own true love!" She threw her arms around Stephen and this time it was his turn to go red.

"You're so *clever* to have taken all that food. You *won't* give it back, will you?"

"Come on, let's go!" said Stephen to Bruce, looking very embarrassed.

"Where you go I follow!" said Mirror-Belle. "The only way to break the spell is to give me a bag of food, but I'm sure you won't want to do that, will you?"

The boys dumped the bag at Mirror-Belle's feet and ran off.

After Mirror-Belle had given the food

back to its owners the skipping game
started up again, this time undisturbed.

"Are those *really* magic crisps?" asked
Katy.

"Try one and see!" said Mirror-Belle.

Katy ate a crisp and so did Ellen, but
neither of them fell in love with anyone.

"Perhaps it only works on princesses,"
said Mirror-Belle.

Back in the classroom the teacher got the paints out and told the children to roll up their sleeves and put aprons on.

"We're going to do a project on pets this term," she said. "I'd like you all to paint a picture of a pet. It can either be your own pet or one belonging to a friend."

Ellen started on a picture of her goldfish. The teacher came over to their table.

"That's good, Ellen," she said. "I like those wiggly water weeds." She looked at Mirror-Belle's paper. "I see you're painting two animals, Mirror-Belle. What are they? A dog and a cat?"

"No," said Mirror-Belle, "a lion and a unicorn."

"What an imagination you've got!"

said the teacher.

"It's not me who's got the imagination, it's them!" said Mirror-Belle. "For some reason they both seem to imagine they should be sitting on the throne instead of my father. They're always fighting for the crown. It's a wonder they haven't torn each other to pieces by now."

But the teacher had stopped listening and was looking instead at Mirror-Belle's

hands and arms. They were covered in yellow splodges.

"You've got an awful lot of paint on yourself, Mirror-Belle," she said.

"Oh dear me," said Mirror-Belle. "That's not paint – I think I'm turning into gold again! I thought I was feeling a bit peculiar. I'll have to have a dip in that magic river before I get solid."

"I'm sure you'll find the tap water in the cloakroom will do the job, Mirror-Belle," the teacher said sternly. "And if you're still feeling peculiar after that you can go to the medical room."

"How could I get there if I've turned to gold?" asked Mirror-Belle, as she left the classroom.

Ten minutes later, when she still hadn't come back, the teacher sent Ellen into the cloakroom. Ellen wasn't surprised at what she found. Mirror-Belle had gone, and the cloakroom mirror was covered in smears of yellow paint. On the floor Ellen found a scrap of paper with some backwards writing on it. She held it up to the mirror and read:

Dear Ellen, Sorry I had to go. Love Mirror-Belle. P.S. Give Bruce Baxter and Stephen Hodge a kiss each from me.

Mirror-Belle never came back to school. The head teacher wrote a letter to Ellen's mum saying, *You only enrolled one child at our school, and we feel that your other child might fit in better somewhere else.* Ellen's mum thought this was rather strange.

"I wasn't thinking of sending Luke to Ellen's school – he's too old, in any case," she said.

Ellen made some friends at school and soon stopped feeling shy. But she never gave Bruce or Stephen their kiss from Mirror-Belle because they didn't come anywhere near her.

Bruce and Stephen weren't taking any chances. The new girl looked normal. As far as they could tell her crisps were normal. She said she was called Ellen. But maybe – just maybe – she was really Mirror-Belle.

Princess
MIRROR-BELLE
and the Magic Shoes

For Alyssa and Brooke

Contents

Chapter One

The Magic Shoes

"Hey, you! Yes, you! Turn around, look over your shoulder," sang Ellen's brother, Luke, into the microphone.

Ellen was sitting in the village hall watching Luke's band, Breakneck, rehearse for the Battle of the Bands. The hall was nearly empty, but that evening it would be packed with fans of the six different bands who were entering the competition.

As well as being Breakneck's singer, Luke wrote most of their songs, including this one.

"It's me! Yes, me! Turn around, I'm

still here," he sang. Then he wandered moodily around the stage, while the lead guitarist, Steph, played a twangy solo.

Steph, who never smiled, wore frayed baggy black trousers with a pointless chain hanging out of the pocket and a black T-shirt with orange flames on it. The solo went on and on.

"Steph's so good at the guitar," Ellen whispered to Steph's sister Seraphina, who was sitting next to her.

"I know," said Seraphina. She was two years older than Ellen and dressed very much like her brother, except that her T-shirt had a silver skull on it. "But I bet they don't win. I don't think they should have chosen this song. It's not going to get people dancing. Steph wrote a much better one called 'Savage'."

Ellen couldn't imagine Steph writing anything dancy, but she was quite shy of Seraphina and didn't say so. Besides, she had just remembered something.

"Dancing – help! I'm going to be late for ballet!" She picked up a bag from the floor.

"You've got the wrong bag – that's mine," said Seraphina, who also went to ballet, but to a later class.

"Sorry." Ellen grabbed her own bag and hurried to the door.

At least she didn't have far to go. The ballet classes were held in a room called the studio, which was above the hall. Ellen ran up the stairs.

The changing room was empty. The other girls must be in the studio already, but Ellen couldn't hear any music so the class couldn't have started yet.

Hurriedly, she put on her leotard and ballet shoes and scooped her hair into the hairnet that Madame Jolie, the ballet teacher, insisted they all wear. Madame Jolie was very fussy about how they looked and could pounce on a girl for the smallest thing, such as crossing the ribbons on her ballet shoes in the wrong way.

Ellen was just giving herself a quick check in the full-length mirror when a voice said, "What's happened to your feet?"

It was a voice that she knew very well.

It was coming from the mirror and it belonged to Princess Mirror-Belle.

Ellen and Mirror-Belle had met several times before. Mirror-Belle looked just like Ellen's reflection, but instead of staying in the mirror as reflections usually do, she had a habit of coming out of it. She was much cheekier and naughtier than Ellen and she was always boasting about her life in the palace and the magic things that she said happened to her.

Ellen hadn't seen Mirror-Belle for a while, and she wasn't sure how pleased she was to see her now. All too often Mirror-Belle had got them both into trouble and then escaped into a mirror, leaving Ellen to take the blame.

"Mirror-Belle! You can't come to my dancing class," she said now, then added, "What do you mean about my feet anyway? What's wrong with them?"

"They're not dancing!" said Princess

Mirror-Belle, leaping out of the mirror into the changing room. She was wearing an identical leotard and ballet shoes to Ellen's, and a hairnet too, though she pulled this off and flung it to the ground with a shudder, saying, "I must have walked through a spider's web." Then she began to prance around the room, pointing her toes and waving her arms.

"Stop! You'll tire yourself out before the class has even started," said Ellen.

"I can't stop. And I'm surprised that you can. I think you should take your shoes back to the elves and complain."

"What elves?" asked Ellen.

But already Mirror-Belle had opened the door to the studio and was dancing in. Ellen followed her with a sinking feeling.

The other girls in the class were standing in a line, waiting to curtsy to Madame Jolie. Ellen and Mirror-Belle joined the line. Some of the girls tittered as Mirror-Belle continued to dance up and down on the spot.

"Who's she?" asked one.

"She looks just like you, Ellen," said another.

Madame Jolie had been talking to the lady who played the piano, but now she turned round to face the class.

"*Bon our, mes élèves*," she said.

This meant "Good day, my pupils," in

French. Madame Jolie was French and she always started the class like this.

"*Bon our, Madame*," chanted Ellen and the other girls as they dropped a curtsy to the teacher – all except Mirror-Belle, who twirled around with her arms above her head.

"Leetle girl on ze left – zat ees not a curtsy," said Madame Jolie.

"Ah, you noticed – well done." Mirror-

Belle jiggled about as she spoke. "No, I *never* curtsy – except very occasionally to my parents, the King and Queen. And I'm surprised that all these girls are curtsying to you instead of to me – or are you a princess too?"

"Zees ees not ze comedy class," replied Madame. Then her frown deepened. "Where ees your 'airnet?" she asked.

"A *hairnet*, did you say? Why on earth should I wear one of those? The only thing I ever put on my head is a crown. I didn't wear one today, though, because . . ." Mirror-Belle paused for a second and then went on, "because one of the diamonds fell out of it yesterday and it had to go to the palace jeweller to be repaired."

Ellen wondered if this was true. She had never seen Mirror-Belle with a crown on and sometimes doubted if she really *was* a princess.

"If you forget ze 'airnet one more time you will leave ze class," warned Madame. Then she ordered the girls to go to the barre.

"We will practise ze *pliés*. First position, everyone."

Ellen and the others held the barre with their right hands and, with their heels together, turned their toes out. Then, as the piano started up, they all bent their knees and straightened up again. Ellen couldn't see Mirror-Belle, who was behind her, but she could hear a thumping sound and some stifled giggles.

"*Non, non, non!*" exclaimed Madame. She clapped her hands to stop the music and then wagged her finger at Mirror-Belle. "Why ees it zat you are jumping? I said plié, not sauté. A plié is a bend. A sauté is a jump." She demonstrated the two movements gracefully.

"It's no use telling me that," said Mirror-Belle, leaving the barre and dancing up to Madame. "It's my ballet shoes you should be talking to."

Some of the girls giggled, but Madame was not impressed. "Do not argue, and keep still!" she ordered Mirror-Belle.

"But I can't!" Mirror-Belle complained. "I did think that *you* might understand about my shoes, even if Ellen doesn't. I can see I'll have to explain."

"Zere is no need for zat," said Madame, but Mirror-Belle ignored her. Skipping around in time to her own words, she said, "They're magic shoes. As soon as I put them on, my feet start dancing and I can't stop till the soles are worn out." She twirled around and then added, "Sometimes I dance all night."

"Then why aren't they worn out already?" asked one of the girls, and received a glare from Madame.

"This is a new pair," said Mirror-Belle. "Some elves crept into the palace and made them for me in the night. I hid behind a curtain and watched them. Luckily they didn't see me. If they found out I knew about them, they'd probably never come back. They're very shy, you see." She leaped in the air and landed with a thump. "This pair is very well made. They'll probably take ages to wear out."

Madame had had enough. "In zat case, you can go and wear zem out somewhere else," she said angrily.

"What a good idea," said Mirror-Belle. "So you're not just a pretty pair of feet after all," and she flitted and twirled her way to the door.

"Come on, Ellen!" she called over her shoulder as she danced out of the room.

Ellen hesitated. Part of her wanted to follow Mirror-Belle, to try to stop her causing too much chaos elsewhere. On the other hand, she never was very good at that; usually she just got drawn into whatever trouble Mirror-Belle created. She decided to stay where she was. With a bit of luck, Mirror-Belle might get bored and go back through the changing-room mirror into her own world.

"What an *enfant terrible*!" muttered Madame. "And no 'airnet!" she added, as if this was the worst crime of all. Then she turned back to the class. "Now, *mes élèves*, we will do ze *pliés* in second position."

Ellen's mother, Mrs Page, was teaching the piano to Robert Rumbold when the doorbell rang.

"Excuse me, Robert," she said, interrupting a piece called "Boogie Woogie Bedbug", which Robert was playing very woodenly. She went to the door.

"Ellen, you're back very early – and why are you still in your dancing things?"

"I'm not Ellen, I'm Princess Mirror-Belle," said the girl on the doorstep. She danced past Ellen's mother and into the sitting room.

"Don't be silly, Ellen. And come out of there. You know you're not allowed in the sitting room when I'm teaching."

Ellen's mother had never met Mirror-Belle before. Although Ellen was always talking about her, her mother thought she was just an imaginary friend.

Robert was still playing "Boogie Woogie Bedbug", and the girl who Mrs Page thought was Ellen was slinking around the room, waggling her hips and clicking her fingers in time to the music.

"You heard me, Ellen. Go to your room and get changed. Where are your clothes anyway?"

"That's a tricky question. It depends on whether my maid is having a lazy day or not. If she is, then my clothes are still on the palace floor where I left them. If she's not, then they're hanging up in the royal wardrobe," said the girl, jumping on to the sofa and off again.

"I suppose you've left them at ballet," said Mrs Page with a sigh. "You'd better go back there now and get changed."

"That's really no way to talk to a princess, but since you're my friend's mother I'll excuse you." She danced out of the room and Ellen's mother heard the front door slam.

"I'm so sorry about that, Robert," she said.

Robert just grunted and went on playing "Boogie Woogie Bedbug". Strangely enough, the piece was now sounding much livelier than before, as if the bedbug had learned to jump at last.

"That's coming on so much better," Mrs Page told him as she saw him out a few minutes later. "Keep practising it, and then next week you can start on 'Hip Hop Hippo'."

Just then she spotted Ellen coming round the corner towards the house. She was wearing her outdoor clothes.

"Hello, Ellen – that was very quick! You're back just in time to apologize to Robert."

"What for?" asked Ellen, looking puzzled.

"For barging in to his lesson like that."

"Oh no, don't say Mirror-Belle's been here," groaned Ellen. "Where is she now?"

"She's in your imagination – just the same as usual – so stop blaming her for everything you do wrong. In fact, if you mention Mirror-Belle one more time I won't let you go to the Battle of the Bands."

That evening Ellen, who had succeeded in not mentioning Mirror-Belle (though she kept thinking about her), was standing near the front of the village hall waiting for the second half of the Battle of the Bands to start. Three of the bands had played already, and the last of these, Hellhole, had received wild applause. Breakneck would have to play really well to beat them.

"Do you want a Coke?" came a voice. It was Seraphina, who had pushed her way through the crowds of people to join Ellen.

"Thanks. I like your T-shirt – it's cool," said Ellen.

Seraphina was no longer wearing her skull T-shirt. This one had a green-winged snake on it.

"Did you hear what happened to my other one?" asked Seraphina. "It was stolen from the changing room while I was at my ballet class. So were my jeans. Who do you think could have taken them?"

"I've no idea," said Ellen untruthfully.

In fact, she had a very strong suspicion. Mirror-Belle must have danced back to the hall while the older girls were having their lesson and changed into Seraphina's black jeans and silver-skull T-shirt. But where was she now?

Just then the lights in the hall were dimmed and some bright-coloured ones came on over the stage.

"Hi there, pop-pickers! Welcome back to the battlefield!" said the compère, Mr Wilks, who was a geography teacher in Luke's school.

Seraphina sniggered. "He's not exactly cool, is he?" she whispered.

Ellen decided she didn't like the superior way in which Seraphina always spoke. Mirror-Belle put on airs too, but at least she could be good fun. Ellen wondered again where she had got to.

"Put your paws together for Breakneck!" said Mr Wilks, and Ellen clapped much louder than anyone else as Luke, Steph and the other members of Breakneck slouched on to the stage.

Luke tripped up on his way to his place and everyone laughed. Ignoring them, he hunched over the microphone.

"Hey, you! Yes, you!" he began.

He was pointing at the audience, and Ellen thought he looked quite good, but she could hear him only very faintly. Then he stopped altogether and signalled to Steph and the others to stop playing. What had gone wrong?

The sound technician came on to the stage, sighed and plugged the lead from Luke's microphone into the amplifier.

"It must have come unplugged when he tripped," said Seraphina.

Not looking too put out, Luke started again.

"Hey, you! Yes, you! Turn around, look over your shoulder," he sang.

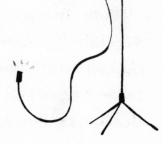

A loud screeching sound accompanied his voice.

"Feedback," whispered Seraphina knowledgeably.

This time, Luke didn't stop. The sound technician fiddled about with a knob and soon Luke's voice sounded normal. In fact, he was singing really well, Ellen thought, though she probably wouldn't admit it to him afterwards. But it had not been a good beginning. Some of the audience were still laughing, and a couple of Hellhole fans tried to start up a chant of, "Get them off!"

Breakneck didn't let any of this upset them. They carried on, and by the time Steph's twangy guitar solo started quite a few people were tapping their feet and swaying. The coloured lights were flashing and some smoke started to rise from the foot of the stage.

"That's the smoke machine," said

Seraphina. "It was Steph's idea."

The guitar solo came to an end at last and Luke started the "Hey, you!" chorus again.

Ellen was aware of a disturbance somewhere behind her.

"Watch out!"

"Stop pushing!"

"That was my toe!"

She turned around and saw who was creating the fuss and bother. It was a girl dressed in black, dancing her way through the crowds. Because she was flinging her arms around, people were making way for her and soon she was at the very front of the hall.

"Turn around," sang Luke, and the girl turned around, her loose hair flying about.

"Look over your shoulder," he sang, and she stuck her chin out over her right shoulder, at the same time stamping her right foot and raising her left hand. Her wild hair was almost covering her face, but Ellen had no doubt who it was.

"Mirror-Belle, how could you?" she muttered under her breath. Just when Breakneck were beginning to impress people . . . This would ruin their chances!

But, to her surprise, a couple of girls in the front row started copying Mirror-Belle's movements, turning around whenever she did, looking over their shoulders with the same stamp and hand gesture, and pointing whenever Luke sang "Hey, you!" Some people stared at them, but others began to join in.

The dance was infectious. Very soon nearly everyone in front of Ellen seemed to be doing it. They were joining in the words of the song as well. She turned round and saw that the people behind her were dancing and singing too.

On the stage, Luke was grinning. He

caught Steph's eye and mouthed something to him. Ellen knew that they were at the end of the song, but they weren't slowing down like they usually did.

"They've gone back to the beginning! They're going to sing it all over again!" she whispered to Seraphina happily.

She expected Seraphina to look happy too, but instead she was staring accusingly at Mirror-Belle.

"Have you seen what I have?" she asked. "She's wearing my clothes! She's the thief!"

She strode forward, pushing through the dancers in front of her and reaching out for the skull T-shirt, which looked more like a dress on Mirror-Belle. Just when Seraphina tried to grab it,

Mirror-Belle did another of her spins and, for the first time, noticed Ellen behind her.

"Oh, hello, Ellen. Why didn't you come with me? I've been visiting your local library. It hasn't got nearly so many books as the palace library, but that's quite good in a way, because it meant there was lots of room for dancing about. I must say, though, some of the servants in there are awfully rude."

So that's where Mirror-Belle had been! Now Ellen would dread going to the library, knowing that the librarians would think she was the naughty dancing girl they had told off.

Meanwhile, the rest of the audience

were so carried away with the song and dance that they didn't spot that Mirror-Belle had stopped doing the actions along with them. They took no more notice of her – apart from Seraphina, that is, who was making another grab at the T-shirt.

Mirror-Belle was too quick for her. "Excuse me," she said, "my shoes are taking off again!" and the next moment she was dancing her way back through the crowds.

Seraphina followed her, and Ellen followed Seraphina. The rest of the audience just went on dancing in time to the music – almost as if they were all wearing magic shoes themselves.

"Where's she gone?"

asked Seraphina.

They were out of the hall now and Mirror-Belle was nowhere to be seen.

"Let's look outside," suggested Ellen.

In fact, she was pretty sure that Mirror-Belle would be on her way to the nearest mirror, the one in the changing room upstairs, but she wanted to give her a little time to escape from Seraphina. She felt a bit guilty about this – after all, Mirror-Belle had taken Seraphina's clothes – but she couldn't help being on Mirror-Belle's side.

They peered out of the front door and up and down the street.

"No," said Seraphina. "Anyway, she wouldn't go outside – she was wearing ballet shoes."

You don't know Mirror-Belle, thought Ellen, but said nothing.

"Let's look upstairs," said Seraphina, and she led the way.

"Look! There are my clothes on the floor!" she cried, as they entered the changing room. She picked them up. "They're drenched in sweat!" she said in disgust. "You'd think she'd been dancing ever since she put them on. Here, you hold them, Ellen – I'm going to find her."

Seraphina strode into the studio, but emerged a few moments later, looking puzzled. "That's funny," she said. "She's not in there, and there's no other way out." Then, "Why are you smiling?" she asked Ellen, who was glancing at the mirror.

Ellen didn't want to tell Seraphina that she knew where Mirror-Belle had gone. She would have to explain her smile some other way.

"I'm smiling," she said, "because I'm sure Breakneck are going to win the Battle of the Bands."

Then she turned back to the mirror

and quietly, so that Seraphina wouldn't hear, she whispered, "Thanks, Mirror-Belle."

Chapter Two

The Golden Goose

"Ooh, look, here comes Dad! Now he's off again – that was quick!" Ellen's granny sounded very excited. She was peering out of the window of the spare bedroom through a pair of binoculars. "He'll be back again in no time, you wait and see . . . Yes, here he is! Good old Dad!"

Granny wasn't talking about Ellen's father, who was away in Paris with her mother, but about a blue tit that was flying in and out of a nesting box in the garden, feeding his young family.

"Here, you have a look, Ellen!"

Granny passed over the binoculars and Ellen trained them on the nesting box, which was hanging from a tree. Sure enough, she saw the little bird fly in through the hole in the box and then out again.

"Keep watching! I'll go and make the tea," said Granny.

Ellen watched the blue tit come and go a few times, then lost interest and started experimenting with the binoculars. She found that if she looked through them the other way round, the tree with the nesting box appeared very small and far away. Everything did. She turned slowly round the bedroom, looking through the binoculars at the tiny bed, chest of drawers and wardrobe. It looked like a bedroom in a doll's house.

"And I'm the doll," she said, peering at her own shrunken reflection in the wardrobe mirror.

"Don't you mean the elephant?" came an answering voice, and out of the mirror jumped a tiny girl with a tiny pair of binoculars of her own. Although she was so small, Ellen recognized her immediately. It was Princess Mirror-Belle.

"Mirror-Belle! You've shrunk!" Removing the binoculars from her eyes, Ellen squatted down to talk to Princess Mirror-Belle, who had climbed on to her shoe.

"Don't be silly – it's you who've grown," replied Mirror-Belle, adding, "I must say, I'm surprised to find you here at all. What

are you doing at the top of a beanstalk?"

"I'm not at the top of a beanstalk," said Ellen. She was about to tell Mirror-Belle that she was at her grandparents' house, staying there for the Easter weekend, when a gruff voice called out, "Ellen! It's teatime!"

"It's the giant!" cried Mirror-Belle, clutching Ellen's ankle in alarm.

"No, it's not – it's Grandpa," said Ellen.

Mirror-Belle took no notice. "You'll have to hide me, Ellen!" she said.

"Oh, all right," said Ellen. "How about in here?" She picked Mirror-Belle up carefully and popped her into the drawer of the bedside table.

"It's much too hard," complained Mirror-Belle. "Not at all suitable for a princess. Can't you line it with velvet, or moss, or something?"

Ellen looked around. There was a box

of tissues on the table. She pulled out a few. "Will these do?" she asked as she set them down in the drawer. Mirror-Belle looked doubtful, but when Grandpa's voice came again – "Ellen! Hurry up!" – she lay down on the tissues.

"Don't forget *my* tea, will you?" she said, as Ellen went out of the room. "Beanstalk-climbing is hungry work."

There were home-made scones for tea. Ellen wanted to sneak one into her pocket for Mirror-Belle, but it was difficult to find the right moment. Granny and Grandpa never seemed to take their attention off her: they kept talking to her about their two favourite subjects – the garden and the birds who visited it.

"Over four hundred daffodils we had this year," said Granny. And, "Wait till you see my new bird bath, Ellen," boasted Grandpa.

It was only when Granny called out, "Look! There they are, the rascals!" that both their heads turned to the window to look at a pair of magpies, and Ellen whisked the scone off her plate and into her pocket.

It was a while before she could give it to Mirror-Belle, since Grandpa insisted on taking her on a tour of the garden first, pointing out with pride the bird bath and the gnomes, which he had carved himself. When Ellen eventually managed to escape to her bedroom, she found Princess Mirror-Belle in a grumpy mood.

"Not very appetizing," she said, giving the scone a disapproving look.

"It's delicious," said Ellen, and broke it into crumbs.

Mirror-Belle seized a handful of crumbs and stuffed them into her mouth. "The palace pastry-cook would get the sack if he produced anything as plain as this," she grumbled, but she ate all the crumbs swiftly and they seemed to improve her mood. "Now," she said, "it's time to look for the golden goose."

"What golden goose?" asked Ellen.

"The one that lays the golden eggs, of course. A giant stole it from the palace and I've come to get it back. I wonder where he's hidden it." Mirror-Belle picked up her tiny binoculars and put them to her eyes the wrong way round.

"You need to look through the other end for spotting birds," said Ellen.

Mirror-Belle looked put out for a second, but then retorted, "I certainly do not. Everything here is terrifyingly huge already. If I made it look any bigger I'd probably die of fright. This is giant land, remember."

Ellen laughed. "Do you think

I'm a giant then?" she asked.

"That's been puzzling me," said Mirror-Belle. "No. I think that the giants must have been fattening you up to eat you. But don't worry, I know how to make a special shrinking potion. Could you get hold of some petrol and shoe polish, and a few spoonfuls of marmalade?"

"*No*," said Ellen. "It would just get me into trouble, like that time in the bathroom."

She was remembering the very first time they had met. Mirror-Belle had appeared out of the bathroom mirror and persuaded Ellen to mix up all sorts of things in the bath.

Mirror-Belle looked slightly disappointed but then said, "While we're on the subject of baths, it's about time that I had mine." She yawned, and added, "And then bed, I think. We can always hunt for the golden goose tomorrow."

So Mirror-Belle was planning to stay the night! Ellen wasn't sure how she felt about that. Still, a bath couldn't do any harm. Ellen pointed to the washbasin in the corner of the bedroom. "Will you have your bath in there?" she asked.

"Good heavens, no!" said Mirror-Belle. "It's the size of the palace swimming pool. Surely you could find me something more suitable." She looked around and then pointed out of the window. "That coconut shell would be just the job. I can't think why it's hanging from a tree."

"I can't get you that," said Ellen. "It's got fat and raisins and things in it, for the birds."

A suspicious look crossed Mirror-Belle's face at the mention of birds. "For the golden goose, perhaps?" she said.

Ellen decided to change the subject back to Mirror-Belle's bath. "I've got a different idea," she said, and left the room.

She tiptoed past the sitting room, where Granny and Grandpa were watching television, and into the kitchen. In a cupboard she found a pretty china sugar bowl with a pattern of bluebells on it. It wasn't the one Granny used every day, and Ellen hoped she wouldn't miss it.

Mirror-Belle was delighted with her flowery china bath. "It's almost as good

as the one in the palace, which has roses and lilies on it," she said. She splashed around happily, and allowed herself to be dried with Ellen's face flannel. Then, "What about my nightdress?" she asked.

"I suppose you'll just have to get back into your clothes," said Ellen, but Mirror-Belle would hear of no such thing. "Can't you make one for me out of rose petals?" she said.

"No," said Ellen. "It's not the time of year for roses, and I'm no good at sewing. Granny is, though," she added, suddenly remembering the clothes-peg dolls she used to play with when she was little, and the dresses Granny made for them.

The dolls used to be kept in an old wooden toy box under the spare-room bed. Ellen knelt down and looked. Yes! The box was still there; she recognized its brass handles. She pulled it out and rummaged inside, while Mirror-Belle shivered and said, "Do hurry up! I'm freezing!"

At the bottom of the box Ellen found the five clothes-peg dolls. She took them out and lifted Mirror-Belle down to the floor to show them to her. Four of the dolls had quite plain cotton dresses, but the fifth had a shiny purple one; Ellen remembered Granny making it from a silk tie that Grandpa didn't like.

Mirror-Belle's eyes lit up and she practically ripped the purple dress off the doll, then pulled it over her own head.

"Now, all that remains to be found is the royal bed," she said. "And I think I've spotted it." She ran under the big bed and climbed into one of Ellen's slippers. "I don't expect the giants will look for me here," she said.

"Would you like one of my socks as a sleeping bag?" asked Ellen, who was beginning to enjoy herself. It was a bit like having the very latest walkie-talkie doll to play with, even though Mirror-Belle was rather a bossy doll. Ellen actually felt disappointed when Granny called her away for a game of cards.

"Don't forget my cocoa!" Mirror-Belle called out after her, but when Ellen came back to the bedroom she was fast asleep.

The following morning Mirror-Belle announced that she was going to search high and low for the golden goose. "It's a good thing I've got you to help me, Ellen," she said. "You can look in all the high-up places."

But Ellen had other plans for the day: Granny and Grandpa had promised to take her out to the local safari park.

Mirror-Belle looked sulky when she heard this, but then her face brightened. "I suppose it's quite cunning of you to get the giants out of the way, so that I can carry out my search in peace," she said.

Ellen began to worry. "You're not to

mess up the house," she warned Mirror-Belle. "And what will you eat and drink all day?"

"You'll have to see to that," said Mirror-Belle. "Whoever heard of a princess getting her own meals?"

Ellen managed to scrounge a few bits of food before she set out with Granny and Grandpa: some Choc-o-Hoops from her own breakfast, a scraping of cheese from the sandwiches Granny was making for their picnic and a couple of grapes from the fruit bowl. She delivered them to Mirror-Belle on a tray that was really the lid of a jam jar, and filled

the cap of her shampoo bottle with water.

"I'd prefer cowslip cordial," said Mirror-Belle.

"Tough," said Ellen, surprising herself by answering back for once. Maybe it was easier than usual because Mirror-Belle was so much smaller than her. Feeling a bit guilty, she said, "I'll try and save you some goodies from the picnic."

Ellen enjoyed the safari park, but she couldn't help worrying what Mirror-Belle might be getting up to. She wished now that she had been hard-hearted enough to close her bedroom door before setting out.

"I'll put the kettle on," said Granny when they got back.

Ellen ran up to her bedroom, feeling relieved that the hall and stairs at least looked the same as when they had left.

"Mirror-Belle!" Ellen called out softly, going into the room and closing the door behind her.

"Nineteen, twenty, twenty-one," came Mirror-Belle's voice.

"I've got you some crisps and some Smarties," said Ellen.

"Be quiet a minute, I'm trying to count." The voice was coming from under the bed. "Twenty-two, twenty-three, twenty-four. The greedy things! This is probably some poor human's life savings."

Ellen lay on her tummy and saw not just Mirror-Belle but a heap of chocolate coins – the kind that are covered in gold paper. An empty little gold net and a pair of gold nail scissors lay beside them.

"Where did

you find those?" she asked.

"Wait till you see what else I've found," said Mirror-Belle, and she ran behind the toy box.

"Not the golden goose, I bet," said Ellen.

"No, but look at this golden hen!" said Mirror-Belle, coming back into view with a little round fluffy Easter chick in her arms. "Unfortunately it seems to be dead," she said as she set it down beside the coins.

"It's not dead, it's just a toy," said Ellen. "I expect Granny and Grandpa were planning to give it to me for Easter – and the coins too. I'll have to put them back wherever you found them. It's a shame you cut the bag open."

Mirror-Belle wasn't listening. She had

picked up the golden net and taken it back behind the toy box. A moment later she reappeared, dragging it after her. "Look at all this stolen treasure!" she said. Grunting with the effort, she emptied the net.

Ellen gasped in horror as out fell two pairs of gold cufflinks, a watch and a diamond ring.

"I'm sure I recognize this crown," said Mirror-Belle, putting the ring on her head with the diamond at the front. "I seem to remember it went missing from the palace a few years ago. And this clock looks familiar too."

"It's not a clock – it's Granny's best watch. And that's her ring, and Grandpa's cufflinks. Oh, Mirror-Belle, this is terrible! Where did you find them all?"

"I'm not telling you. You'll only

go and put them back," said Mirror-Belle.

"Yes, of course I will. Straight away, before Granny and Grandpa miss them. Go on, Mirror-Belle – you *must* tell me."

"Oh, very well," said Mirror-Belle, who was obviously finding it difficult to resist boasting about her skill as an explorer. "The coins and the golden hen were easy enough to find – they were in a bag under the giants' bed. But the treasure and the golden shears were another matter."

"What golden shears? Oh, you mean the scissors. Where were they?"

"I was just about to tell you. It's a good thing the beanstalk had given me so much climbing practice – though I must say, the white snake was even more difficult."

"What white snake? What are you talking about, Mirror-Belle? Do explain properly!"

"It wasn't actually a snake, I suppose — more of a long, slippery white rope, leading to the giants' treasure chest."

"I think you must mean a light flex," said Ellen. "Right, I'm off."

She scooped up everything that Mirror-Belle had collected.

"Stop! Whose side are you on?" Mirror-Belle protested, but Ellen ignored her.

Making sure to close the door behind her this time, she crept along the landing and into her grandparents' bedroom. She could hear Granny calling her to tea, but she had to put the things back first.

Sure enough, there was a carrier bag under the bed. Inside it were a couple of boxes which must contain Easter eggs. Ellen slipped the fluffy chick and the bag of coins in beside them.

The "white snake" was, as she had suspected, the flex of Granny's bedside lamp. Beside the lamp was a round embroidered jewel box with an unzipped lid. Ellen put the ring, watch and cuff-links inside. She wasn't sure exactly where the scissors belonged but she put them down beside the box and hoped for the best.

Just then she heard footsteps on the stairs.

"Ellen! Where are you? Your tea's getting cold."

Ellen's heart was thumping. If Granny found her here, how would she explain what she was doing? She stood frozen, wondering whether to hide. Then she heard Granny tap at the door of the spare bedroom and go in.

Quickly and quietly, Ellen went downstairs and into the kitchen, where Grandpa was having his tea.

"Your gran's looking for you," he said, and a moment later Granny came in.

"That's funny . . . Oh, there you are, Ellen. Where have you been?"

Ellen muttered something about the bathroom. Granny didn't look too pleased, and Ellen noticed that she was holding the sugar basin in one hand. In her other hand was the jam-jar lid, containing some grape pips and a little bit of cheese.

"What's all this?" said Granny. "Am I not feeding you enough?"

Ellen felt herself go red, but Grandpa said, "Don't scold the lass. I bet she was having a dolls' tea party, weren't you, Ellen?"

Ellen agreed, even though she was too old for that sort of thing. She didn't like lying to her kind grandparents, but it seemed the best way out of a tricky situation.

Granny had made a delicious fruitcake, but Ellen decided against smuggling any of it out to Mirror-Belle. Instead, she would try to persuade her mirror friend to go home.

"You'll have to, Mirror-Belle," she told her after tea. "I can't get you any more food, and Granny's taken your bath back, and . . . well, you must realize that you're not going to find the golden goose."

But Mirror-Belle refused to give up. "Tomorrow I search the garden," she said. "Now, what flavour were those crisps you were telling me about, Ellen? I hope they're smoky dragon ones."

The next day was Easter Sunday. There was a big Easter egg for Ellen on the breakfast table, along with the fluffy chick and the bag of chocolate money.

"I'm sorry the bag broke open," said Granny. "It looked all right in the shop."

"Stop fussing. The lass doesn't mind," said Grandpa. He turned to Ellen and handed her a piece of paper. "Look what the Easter rabbit left in the garden," he said.

When she was little Ellen had believed in the Easter rabbit, but now she knew that it was Granny and Grandpa who hid the little eggs in the garden every year, with clues to help find them. The piece of paper would be the first clue. She unfolded it and read, in Grandpa's handwriting:

Red-y   n your marks, get set!
Come and get your feathers wet!

She was rather surprised that Grandpa couldn't spell the word "ready" – he had left out the "a" – but was too polite to mention it.

"You'd better start looking if you want to beat those magpies to it," said Granny. "You know how they love anything shiny."

Ellen was about to run outside when she remembered Mirror-Belle. This could be a good opportunity for her to search the garden and discover that there was no golden goose hidden there after all.

"I'll just put on a cardigan," she said, and went up to her bedroom.

Mirror-Belle was still in her purple silk nightdress, lying in the slipper bed.

"You're interrupting my beauty sleep," she complained when Ellen picked her up. But as soon as she heard the plan she stopped fussing. "I'll need my binoculars," she said, so Ellen gave them to her and she snuggled down into the pocket of Ellen's thick, knitted cardigan.

Once they were outside, Mirror-Belle

peeped out over the top of the pocket. "Where are you going?" she asked Ellen.

"To the bird bath," said Ellen. "This first clue's easy."

Sure enough, on the rim round the bird bath she found seven little eggs. They were all wrapped in red shiny paper, which explained Grandpa's funny spelling of the word "ready".

There was a piece of paper beside the eggs, and on it Ellen read the next clue:

Seven others, bright and blue,
In a nutshell wait for you.

"That's easy too!" she said, and went straight to the half-coconut which Mirror-Belle had wanted as her bath. Inside it were seven blue eggs.

"Excuse me," said Mirror-Belle, "but why are we hunting for eggs? I thought we were supposed to be finding the goose." Then she looked thoughtful. "Of course, it would be a different matter if we found some *golden* eggs. Then I could take one home and hatch it into a golden goose."

"It looks as though the next lot are green," said Ellen, and she read out the clue she had found in the coconut shell:

Small green eggs tell small old man,
"Try and catch us if you can."

Ellen was puzzled at first, and Mirror-Belle said, "That's ridiculous. Eggs can't talk and, anyway, there aren't any small men in giant land."

"I've got it!" Ellen cried. "It must mean one of Grandpa's garden gnomes." One gnome had a wheelbarrow and another was smoking a pipe. Ellen searched around them but couldn't find any eggs. Then, "How stupid of me!" she said, and ran towards the fish pond.

"Slow down! I'm getting pocket-sick!" protested Mirror-Belle.

Standing beside the pond stood a garden

gnome with a fishing rod, and at his feet were seven green eggs.

"That's why the clue says, 'Catch us if you can,'" explained Ellen. "Do you want to hear the next one?"

"If you insist," said Mirror-Belle with a yawn.

So Ellen read it out:

In the glass you may behold
Seven eggs of shiny gold.

Mirror-Belle stopped yawning. "The golden eggs!" she cried, and tried to climb out of Ellen's pocket.

"I wonder what 'the glass' means," said Ellen. "I think it could be a pane of the greenhouse."

"Nonsense!" said Mirror-Belle. "It's clearly referring to a mirror."

"But there aren't any mirrors in the

garden," objected Ellen.

"I wouldn't be so sure," said Mirror-Belle, who was much more interested in the egg-hunt now that the next lot of eggs promised to be golden ones. "If you'd only put me down I'm sure that I'd find them in no time."

"All right," said Ellen, "but do be careful." She put Mirror-Belle down at the gnome's feet and said, "I'll see you back here in five minutes." Then she headed for the greenhouse, while Mirror-Belle ran off in the opposite direction.

There weren't any eggs inside the greenhouse. Ellen had just started looking around the outside of it when she heard a triumphant cry: "I've found them!"

Mirror-Belle was standing at the far end of the garden, holding a golden egg above her head. Ellen was surprised at how far she had travelled.

"I'm coming!" she called, and then she saw something else. A magpie was flying down from a tree just above Mirror-Belle. It must have spotted her and decided she could be good to eat.

"Watch out!" Ellen yelled, and started to run. She saw the magpie land and then take off again. Was Mirror-Belle in its beak? She couldn't see.

Ellen reached the spot where she had seen Mirror-Belle. There on the ground was a cluster of golden eggs. She didn't count them, but instead looked round for Mirror-Belle.

"Well? What did you think of the clues?"said Granny. She crossed the lawn and took the piece of paper from Ellen's hand. "That's quite a good one," she said. "Did you spot Grandpa's secret mirror?"

"No," said Ellen. "Where is it?"

Granny pointed at a plant covered in pink flowers. It was a moment before Ellen saw the curved mirror which was standing behind it.

"Another of Grandpa's brainwaves," said Granny. "He was always disappointed that that peony didn't have more flowers, but this way it looks as if it's got twice the amount."

Ellen smiled – not at Grandpa's trick, but because she realized that Mirror-Belle must have disappeared safely into the mirror and not been caught by the magpie after all.

"Did you find all the eggs, then?" asked Granny.

"I think so," said Ellen, and displayed them proudly.

Granny counted them. "There's one missing," she said. "There should be seven of each colour, but you've only found six gold ones." She looked all around the peony and then gave up. "It must be those magpies!" she said.

"Yes, of course," said Ellen, but she knew that even if they found and searched the magpies' nest the missing golden egg would not be in it. Princess Mirror-Belle must have taken it back to mirror land with her. It was only a chocolate egg really, but Ellen couldn't help hoping that it would hatch into a golden goose.

Chapter Three

Prince Precious Paws

"Good, Splodge. Good dog."

For the twentieth time that morning, Ellen picked up the boring-looking stick which lay at her feet. Splodge was gazing up at her with what she called his "Again" look.

"All right, then." Ellen strolled a little way along the lakeside path and then hurled the stick as hard as she could. It landed with a splash in the lake.

In a brown-and-white flash, Splodge was at the water's edge. But there he stopped.

"Go on, Splodge – get it!"

Ellen felt like jumping in herself, the lake looked so cool and inviting under the hot blue sky. But Splodge seemed to have forgotten all about the stick. He was staring into the rippled water and barking. What had he seen? Ellen looked down too. The ripples were clearing now, but all she could see was Splodge's reflection – and her own.

Suddenly the water at their feet started to churn, whirling and splashing as if some huge fish were writhing about in it.

The next second another brown-and-white dog was shaking itself all over Ellen. Splodge barked, and in reply the new dog trotted up and sniffed his bottom. Ellen laughed, then turned to watch as the two dogs chased each other about on the grass.

She was startled by a voice from behind her.

"Didn't you bring a towel? I'm soaking."

Ellen spun round and there, standing up to her knees in water, was Mirror-Belle. She had a dog lead in her hand and wore a stripy dress just like Ellen's, except that it was dripping wet.

"Mirror-Belle! What are you doing here? I thought you only came out of mirrors!" said Ellen. "Though I suppose the lake *is* a kind of mirror."

"We've been diving for treasure,"

replied Mirror-Belle.

Ellen was puzzled at first. Why had Mirror-Belle said "we" instead of "I"? But then the new dog bounded up to Mirror-Belle, nearly knocking her over. With his paws on her chest, he started to lick her face.

"I didn't know you had a dog too," said Ellen.

"Yes," said Mirror-Belle, in between licks. "His name is Prince Precious Paws."

Ellen thought this was rather a silly name but she was too polite to say so. "He looks just like my dog, Splodge," she said. "Does he like fetching sticks too?"

"Certainly not," said Mirror-Belle, as if she had never heard of such a thing. "Why would he want to fetch sticks when he can find rubies and emeralds?"

"Can he really?"

"Of course. How else do you suppose he helped the little tailor to seek his fortune?"

"What are you talking about? What little tailor? I thought you said he was your dog," said Ellen.

Before Mirror-Belle could launch into an explanation, Splodge – keen for more action and less talk – dropped a new stick at Ellen's feet. She was about to pick it up when Prince Precious Paws seized it and growled.

"You told me he didn't like sticks," said Ellen. She looked accusingly at Mirror-Belle, and Splodge looked accusingly at Prince Precious Paws.

Just then a woman with a pushchair came up to Mirror-Belle.

"You poor thing, did you fall in?" she asked. "I hope your twin sister didn't push you!"

"Ellen's not my twin," said Mirror-Belle indignantly. "I'm a princess and she's just an ordinary girl."

"There's a towel in here somewhere,"

said the woman, rummaging in a bag. "William was going to go paddling but now he's fallen asleep in the pushchair."

As she took out the towel, a ball fell from the bag and rolled towards the water. Both dogs went after it, but Ellen called Splodge back.

"Come, Splodge! Sit!" she said, and Splodge came back obediently and sat at her feet.

Mirror-Belle's dog, however, seized the ball and started chewing it savagely, as if it was a rat he was trying to kill.

"Can you make him bring it back, please?" said the woman. "That's William's new ball and he'd be upset if your dog punctured it."

"I'm surprised you let your child play with such a flimsy toy," said Mirror-Belle. "Personally, I only ever play with a golden ball."

"Just call him back, will you?" said the

woman impatiently.

"Very well." Mirror-Belle raised her voice. "Come, Prince Precious Paws, come!" she cried.

But Prince Precious Paws only growled and rested a paw on the ball.

"He's not very obedient, is he?" said the woman.

"Yes, he is – he's just a bit deaf," said Mirror-Belle. "You see, the tailor who owned him had two other dogs as well. These other two had such terribly loud barks that poor Prince Precious Paws's hearing was affected. So when I said 'Come', he probably thought I was saying 'Hum', and that's why he's making that noise."

As if in agreement, Prince Precious Paws began to growl even louder. It was a fierce sound, not like a hum at all, Ellen thought.

"I've never heard such nonsense," said

the woman. "Look! Now he's ripping poor William's ball apart. I really think you should take him to dog-training classes. Your other dog seems to be very well trained. Are they from the same litter?"

"Of course not," said Mirror-Belle. "Prince Precious Paws is a royal dog. He lives in a kennel lined with dia-monds and pearls. Shall I tell you how he came to be mine?"

"No, thank you," said the woman. "I'm going to take William home before he wakes up and makes a fuss." And, snatching her towel back from Mirror-Belle, she strode off angrily.

Ellen felt embarrassed, and sorry for William, though she supposed that his mother would buy him a new ball. She thought about scolding Mirror-Belle, but perhaps it wasn't her fault that Prince Precious Paws was so badly behaved. Probably his previous owner hadn't brought him up properly.

"You can tell *me* if you like," she said, sitting down on a log by the lake. "How you got your dog, I mean."

Mirror-Belle sat down beside Ellen. Her dress and hair were already much drier, thanks to the hot sun and the woman's towel.

"Prince Precious Paws used to belong to a poor old woman," she began.

"I thought you said he belonged to a little tailor."

"That was later. The little tailor didn't have any dogs to start off with. All he had was a bit of bread and cheese in

a red spotty handkerchief. He was seeking his fortune, you see. But then he met the poor old woman and gave her some of the bread and cheese, and in return for his kindness she gave him three dogs. They all had eyes as big as saucers."

"Are you sure?" asked Ellen.

She couldn't actually see Prince Precious Paws's eyes at that moment, as he was bounding away from them across the grass, pursued by Splodge, but as far as she remembered they were no bigger than Splodge's eyes.

Mirror-Belle ignored the interruption. "Luckily for the tailor," she continued, "the three dogs were all brilliant at finding treasure. They kept finding it, in taverns and caves and all sorts of places, and in the end the tailor arrived at the palace with a great sackful of treasure and asked to marry the King's daughter."

"That's you, isn't it?" said Ellen. "But

you're much too young to get married."

"Exactly," said Mirror-Belle. "So I said I'd take one of the dogs instead."

"What happened to the tailor?" asked Ellen, but she didn't find out, because at that moment they heard some angry shouting and saw Prince Precious Paws bounding towards them with something in his mouth. Behind him ran several people, including a man with glasses and a camera who looked vaguely familiar.

Ellen was relieved to see that her own dog was no longer with Prince Precious Paws but was scrabbling about under a nearby tree, probably looking for yet another stick.

"I'll just see what Splodge is up to," she said, and – feeling rather cowardly – she left Mirror-Belle to face the angry people on her own.

"Your dog's stolen our roast chicken!" she heard the man with the camera complain, and suddenly Ellen recognized him. He was Mr Spalding, a science teacher at her brother Luke's school. Mr Spalding ran a Saturday nature-study club called the Sat Nats. The club was open to adults and teenagers. A couple of the keener members of Luke's class – the ones he called the "geeks" – were members, but Luke himself preferred lying in bed on Saturday mornings.

The other Sat Nats were joining in with Mr Spalding now.

"He knocked over the lemonade."

"He's ruined our picnic."

"I don't call that much of a picnic," replied Mirror-Belle. "One measly roast chicken and a bottle of lemonade! I can assure you, Prince Precious Paws is used to far grander picnics than that. He was probably expecting roast swan and champagne."

A couple of the Sat Nats laughed at this, but not Mr Spalding. "Make him drop the chicken," he ordered.

To Ellen's surprise, Mirror-Belle did say, "Drop it, Prince Precious Paws," in a commanding voice, but Prince Precious Paws took no notice and just started swinging the chicken from side to side.

"He's rather deaf, poor creature," Mirror-Belle explained. "He probably thought I said 'rock it'."

This just made Mr Spalding even angrier. He took a photograph of Prince Precious Paws with the chicken and said he would show it to Mirror-Belle's parents. "Where do you live?" he asked her.

"In the palace, of course," she replied, "and I very much doubt if the guards would let you in. You don't exactly look like royalty. Oh, and whatever you do, don't try picnicking in the palace grounds. That's strictly forbidden."

"I know where she lives, sir," chipped in a teenage Sat Nat. "She's Luke Page's little sister."

Ellen's heart sank.

"I am no one of the sort," Mirror-Belle objected, but Mr Spalding seemed satisfied.

He led the Sat Nats back to the remains of their picnic.

"What an impertinent little man," remarked Princess Mirror-Belle, joining Ellen under the tree.

Ellen knew it would be useless to point out who had actually been the impertinent one. Instead, she fastened Splodge's lead to his collar. "I think I'd better take him home now," she said.

"But we haven't found any treasure yet," protested Mirror-Belle. "I'm convinced that Prince Precious Paws is on the brink of a major discovery."

"Where is he?" asked Ellen.

They both looked around, but Mirror-Belle's dog was nowhere in sight.

"He's lost!" cried Mirror-Belle. "What a catastrophe! I shall have to offer a reward to whoever finds him. Do you think a chest of gold would be enough, or should I offer half my father's kingdom?"

"Why don't we just look for him ourselves?" said Ellen. "He can't have gone far. Let's walk round the lake and call him."

So that is what they did, although Ellen half wished she hadn't suggested it, because she felt so stupid calling out "Prince Precious Paws!" time after time.

"Can't we just call 'Prince'?" she suggested to Mirror-Belle.

"Absolutely not. Prince Precious Paws would never answer to such a common name. In fact, he'd probably run a mile in the other direction."

In the end it was Splodge who picked up the scent. He led the two girls away from the lake along a path which took them over a stile and into a field.

"Oh, no," said Ellen. "We're out of the park now. This is a farm. I hope your dog doesn't chase sheep."

"Only if they're wolves in disguise," said Mirror-Belle, which didn't make Ellen feel much better.

 In fact, there were no farm animals in the field, but as they crossed it Ellen heard a loud bleating chorus coming from over the hedge. They climbed another stile and there, huddled in a corner of the next field, was a flock of

terrified-looking sheep. Barking as loudly as the sheep were bleating, and making little runs at them, was Prince Precious Paws.

Splodge pulled on the lead and barked. Prince Precious Paws turned and – almost as if to say, "Your turn now"– bounded away into yet another field.

"I hope we don't meet the farmer," said Ellen, keeping Splodge tightly on the lead as they followed Prince Precious Paws. When they caught up with him, he was barking down a hole in a bank of earth.

"It's probably the entrance to an underground cave full of priceless jewels," said Mirror-Belle.

Ellen thought it looked more like the entrance to a rabbit warren, but you never knew. Prince Precious Paws seemed very excited. His tail was wagging and his precious paws were scrabbling away in the earth. Now his head was half inside the hole and he seemed to be tugging at something.

"It could be the handle of a treasure chest," said Mirror-Belle.

"Or maybe some Roman remains," suggested Ellen, growing quite excited herself. "Luke went on a dig near here once and found part of an ancient vase with pictures of dancers on it."

Just then, Prince Precious Paws growled and his head emerged from the hole. He shook the earth from the object in his jaws. It wasn't a treasure chest or a Roman vase.

"It's a dirty old sheep's skull," said Ellen.

"Oh, good," said Mirror-Belle.

"What's so good about it?"

Mirror-Belle thought for a moment and then said, "Haven't you heard of the legendary sheep with the golden fleece? Its bones are obviously buried here. That means that the golden fleece itself must be nearby – probably hanging from a tree and guarded by a fierce dragon. Prince Precious Paws will find it soon – just wait and see."

"I'm afraid I can't," said Ellen. "I've got to go home for lunch."

She had spotted a gate leading to the road that would take her back home.

"I'll catch up with you as soon as we've found the golden fleece," said

Mirror-Belle, though Ellen rather hoped she wouldn't.

Ellen was just setting off down the road with Splodge when a voice stopped her in her tracks.

"It's that dog again!"

She peeped over the hedge and saw Mr Spalding climbing over the stile into the field, followed by his troop of poor hungry Sat Nats.

"He's still not on the lead!"

"What's that he's got?"

"It's a sheep's skull, isn't it, Mr Spalding? He must have killed one of the sheep and eaten it!"

Ellen didn't stop to hear more, but hurried on with Splodge. It was quite a long walk and she was going to be late for lunch. They were just coming to the place where the road bent sharply and led towards the village when she heard footsteps. She turned and saw Mirror-Belle running towards her. Prince Precious Paws was on the lead at last, and was tugging her along at an amazing speed.

"Can't stop, must fly," Mirror-Belle greeted Ellen as they overtook her and went careering round the bend.

"Watch out, that's a dangerous corner!" Ellen called after them.

When she and Splodge rounded the same bend a minute later, there was no sign of Mirror-Belle or her dog. Although they'd been going so fast, Ellen hadn't expected them to be out of sight already. But then she noticed the mirror by the roadside. It was there so that drivers could see what was coming round the corner. Mirror-Belle and Prince Precious Paws must have disappeared into it.

*

The next day, Luke was practising his electric guitar in his bedroom when the doorbell rang. No one else seemed to be in, so reluctantly he went to the door and was surprised to see his science teacher standing outside.

"Good afternoon, Luke. Are either of your parents in?"

"No, they're not," said Luke, feeling suddenly guilty, as if his teacher somehow knew he hadn't started on his science homework yet.

"Don't worry, this isn't about school," said Mr Spalding, and Luke relaxed a little. He guessed that his teacher must be trying to recruit new members for the Sat Nats.

"I'd really like to join your club, Mr Spalding, but I'm usually rather busy on Saturday mornings, doing my homework, and . . . er . . . taking the dog for a walk."

Hearing his favourite word, Splodge

appeared in the hallway, his lead in his mouth.

"Here's the culprit himself," said Mr Spalding. "That dog is badly in need of training."

Luke started to protest, but Mr Spalding reached into his pocket and handed him two photographs.

"Stealing food and running about off the lead on a sheep farm. Would you call that the behaviour of a well-trained dog?"

Luke studied the photographs. One showed a brown-and-white dog with what looked like a roast chicken in his jaws. In the other picture, the same dog was proudly resting his paw on a sheep skull.

Luke frowned, but then his face cleared.

"You've made a mistake, Mr Spalding. You see, we call our dog Splodge because of the brown splodges on his side and over his eye."

"Exactly. And there they are in the pictures – there's no denying it."

"But Splodge's marks are on his right side and over his left eye – look, you can see. This dog's marks are on his left side and over his right eye."

Mr Spalding looked from the photographs to Splodge and back again. "You're quite right . . . But the girl he was with looked just like your sister . . . It's most extraordinary."

"Don't worry, Mr Spalding. We all make mistakes sometimes," said Luke graciously.

"Well, I do apologize. And perhaps I should apologize to you, old chap," said Mr Spalding, patting Splodge rather timidly on the head.

Luke wondered if Splodge knew he had been wrongly accused. Maybe he even knew who the mystery dog was. But Splodge just gazed up at Mr Spalding with his usual trusting expression. Whatever he knew, he was keeping quiet about it.

Chapter Four

Which Witch?

"Two witches flew out on a moonlit night.

Their laughs were loud and their eyes were
   bright.

Their chins and their noses were pointed
   and long.

They shared the same broom and they
   sang the same song.

Their hats and their cloaks were as black
   as pitch,

And nobody knew which witch was which."

It was Halloween. Ellen, dressed up as
a witch, was practising the poem she
was planning to go round reciting with

her friend Katy.

Most of Ellen's other friends were going out trick-or-treating, but Ellen's mum disapproved of that. She said that in Scotland, where she grew up, children had to recite a poem or tell a joke to earn their Halloween treats. So that was what Ellen and Katy were going to do. It was called guising.

Downstairs, Mum was teaching the piano. One of her star pupils was playing a fast piece whose tune kept going very low and then very high. It reminded Ellen of a witch swooping and soaring on her broomstick, and made her feel excited.

The phone rang. Ellen answered it, and a snuffly Katy said, "It's so unfair. My mum won't let me go out, just because my cold's got worse."

"Oh, poor you," said Ellen, but it was herself she really felt sorry for. As she put the phone down, all her excitement vanished. What was she going to do? She didn't feel like going out on her own, and anyway the poem was supposed to be recited by two identical witches. But now it was too late to ask anyone else to go with her. She would just have to stay at home. What a waste of all the trouble she had taken over her costume – sewing silver stars on to the cloak, spraying glitter on the hat and carving a face out of her pumpkin lantern. She glanced wistfully at herself in the mirror.

"What's the matter? Don't tell me you've lost your cat," came a familiar voice, and a witchy Princess Mirror-Belle stepped out of the mirror, shedding glitter and flourishing her wand.

For once, Ellen was delighted to see her. "What good timing!" she greeted Mirror-Belle. "Now we can go guising together!"

"Disguising is not for the likes of me," said Mirror-Belle. "Your costume may be a disguise, but I really *am* a witch."

"I said *guising*, not disguising," said Ellen, "and anyway, how can you be a witch when you're always telling me you're a princess?"

"Of course I'm a princess," replied Mirror-Belle. "But a wicked ogre has turned me into a witch. A *royal* witch, of course," she added hastily.

"Why did he do that?"

"Because my golden ball landed in his garden and he saw me climbing over his wall to get it back."

"If you're a real witch, can you actually fly that broomstick?" asked Ellen hopefully. Mirror-Belle was holding a small twiggy broomstick just the same as her own.

"Unfortunately, the rotten wizard refused to give me a cat, and everyone knows that a broomstick won't fly without a cat on it. I was hoping that I could borrow your cat, but you seem to have let it escape."

"I never had one," said Ellen. "Anyway, Mirror-Belle, do please come guising with me. I'll teach you the poem, and then we can go round the houses and people will give us lots of goodies."

Mirror-Belle's eyes lit up at the mention of goodies and, after a quick rehearsal of the poem, she followed Ellen downstairs. The impressive sounds of Mum's star pupil were still drifting out of the sitting room.

Ellen found them each a carrier bag. "These are to collect the goodies," she explained. "Mum says we're only to go to people we know and only in this block."

They stepped out into the night.

"Let's start here," said Mirror-Belle, marching up to the house next door.

"No, number 17's been empty since the Johnsons moved out," Ellen told her. "We'll go to the Elliots'."

Mr and Mrs Elliot were the elderly couple who lived two doors along and always had a supply of old-fashioned sweets like pear drops and humbugs and bullseyes.

Mrs Elliot opened the door. She pretended to be scared. "Oh, help!' I'd better let you in quickly, before you turn me into a toad," she said.

"Yes, that would be a good idea," Mirror-Belle agreed.

Mrs Elliot showed them into the cosy front room, where her husband was sitting in an armchair by the fire.

Ellen and Mirror-Belle recited their poem, and Ellen was pleased at how well Mirror-Belle remembered it.

"And nobody knew which witch was which," they finished up. At least, it was supposed to be the end, but Mirror-Belle carried on with another two lines:

"But one of the two was in fancy dress
    While the other was really a royal
    princess."

Mr Elliot chuckled, and Mrs Elliot said, "You've definitely earned your bullseyes."

"I'd rather have some newts' eyes, if you don't mind," said Mirror-Belle. "They're better for spells."

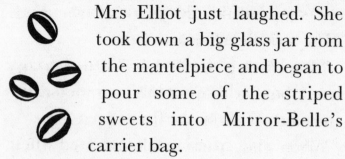

Mrs Elliot just laughed. She took down a big glass jar from the mantelpiece and began to pour some of the striped sweets into Mirror-Belle's carrier bag.

"These don't look like eyes to me," Mirror-Belle complained. "They're just boiled sweets. How are we supposed to do any magic with them?"

Ellen glared at her, but the Elliots laughed again, as if Mirror-Belle had been performing another party piece.

Mr Elliot beckoned them over and handed them two fifty-pence pieces.

"Oh, I see," said Mirror-Belle. "You're expecting us to go to the eye shop ourselves." Then she studied her coin. "I don't think any decent

eye shop would accept this," she said. "The writing is back to front."

"Stop being so cheeky," Ellen muttered, but Mr Elliot roared with laughter and said, "This beats the telly any day."

When they were back outside, Ellen ticked Mirror-Belle off again. "I know the Elliots thought it was funny, but other people might not," she said. "And I don't want to get Katy into trouble. Remember that people probably think you're her."

"But it's so puzzling," said Mirror-Belle. "What do witches want with sweets and money? Surely we should be collecting things like frogs' legs and vampires' teeth?" Then a thoughtful look crossed her face. "Oh, I understand," she said. "Well, we'd better get a move on. We're going to need a huge amount of sweets."

Ellen didn't really see why, but she wasn't in the mood for listening to a long, fanciful explanation, so she was relieved to see Mirror-Belle striding up the path of the next house and ringing on the bell.

An hour or so later, their carrier bags were full of sweets, biscuits, fruit and money.

"Shall we go back to my house?" Ellen suggested to Mirror-Belle, who had been remarkably well behaved – apart from adding the extra two lines to the poem every time they recited it.

"I don't think we'll need to do that," said Mirror-Belle mysteriously.

Before Ellen could ask what she meant, she was striding off again.

"Where are you going?" asked Ellen, trying to catch up.

"In here," said Mirror-Belle, and

pointed her wand at the doors of the mini-supermarket at the end of the road. The doors swung open, as they always did, but she turned and gave Ellen a triumphant look as if she had performed some magic.

Mirror-Belle took a trolley. She dumped her wand and broomstick in it and hung her lantern and carrier bag on the hook at the back. Then she pushed it swiftly up the first aisle to the meat counter at the far end of the shop. Ellen had a horrible feeling that she was going to start demanding newts' eyes and frogs' legs, but instead Mirror-Belle turned her back on the counter and began to recite the poem at the top of her voice.

There weren't many customers in the shop and, to Ellen's relief, no one took much notice. But her relief faded when Mirror-Belle, having finished her version of the poem on a note of triumph, pushed her trolley down the next aisle and started filling it with sweets.

"You can't just take all of those!" Ellen protested, as Mirror-Belle threw in a dozen bags of toffees.

"I agree it would have been polite of someone to offer them to us — not to mention loading the trolley — but unfortunately there's not a servant in sight," said Mirror-Belle, emptying the shelves of liquorice allsorts and reaching for the jelly babies. "It would be quicker if you'd help me," she added.

Ellen tried to think of something to say that would stop Mirror-Belle, but she knew from experience how difficult this was. In any case, the trolley was nearly full now and Mirror-Belle seemed satisfied with her haul.

"Come on," she said, and made her way to one of the checkouts. But instead of stopping and taking the sweets out, she sailed on through.

"Stop!" cried Ellen.

Mirror-Belle was about to push the trolley outside when a shop assistant ran after her and grabbed it.

Ellen felt terrified. What if they were both arrested for shoplifting?

"You haven't paid for this lot, have you?" said the assistant.

"Certainly not," replied Mirror-Belle. "Has it escaped your attention that this is Halloween and that Ellen and I are guising?"

"Not in here, you're not," the shop assistant said firmly.

Mirror-Belle turned to Ellen. "Shall we turn this rude servant into a black beetle?" she suggested.

The shop assistant ignored her and steered the trolley firmly back to the checkout.

"You either pay for them or put them back," he said.

"It's extremely lucky for you that my wand is buried under all the sweets," Mirror-Belle told him. "Poor Ellen here isn't a real witch like me, so she can't do the black-beetle spell."

Ellen could see that Mirror-Belle was just making the assistant angrier and she was scared that he might phone the police. She had to make Mirror-Belle see sense!

"Listen, Mirror-Belle," she said. "We did collect quite a lot of money. If you're so keen for more sweets, perhaps we can buy some of them."

Mirror-Belle sighed. "Very well," she said, "if you think it will stop the servants rioting."

They had enough money for five bags of toffees, four each of liquorice allsorts and jelly babies, and six packets of chewing gum.

"But we'll be sick if we eat all these as well as the sweets and chocolates people gave us," Ellen objected as they left the shop.

"Eat them, did you say? *Eat* them?" Mirror-Belle laughed, as if the idea were absurd. "Where would we live if we ate them?"

"What are you talking about?"

"I'm afraid you're not very well informed about witches, Ellen. Didn't you know that they always live in houses made of sweets?"

Ellen thought about this. "I know that

the witch in 'Hansel and Gretel' had a house of sweets – or was it gingerbread? – but I can't think of any others."

"Where will we build it, I wonder," mused Mirror-Belle, ignoring Ellen and marching back the way they had come. "I know! In the garden of that empty house."

"Mirror-Belle, don't be silly. We haven't got nearly enough sweets to build a house. And anyway, how would we stick them all together?"

"Chewing gum!" said Mirror-Belle, popping a piece into her mouth. "Ah, here we are."

They had reached the empty house, and she opened the tall side gate which led into the overgrown back garden. Ellen followed her nervously.

"Oh, how thoughtful of somebody," said Mirror-Belle, pointing at a large shed in the corner of the garden. "Someone's built it for us already. We'll only need to decorate it."

At first Ellen just watched as Mirror-Belle started to stick jelly babies round one of the shed windows. But it did look rather good fun and soon she was joining in.

"Black, white, pink, yellow,"

she muttered,
as she created a
coloured pattern with liquorice allsorts round the other window. She was standing back to admire the effect when the garden gate creaked and began to open.

"Someone's coming!" she hissed. She pulled Mirror-Belle behind the shed, but couldn't stop her peeping round the edge.

"I think it's the delivery men, come to furnish our new house," said Mirror-Belle. "But surely we don't need two televisions?"

She hadn't lowered her voice, but luckily it was drowned by a crash and a curse from the garden.

Ellen couldn't resist a peep herself. Although the garden was dark, she could make out two men, one carrying a television and another picking up a second television from the ground. Both of them were wearing balaclava helmets over their heads, so that only their eyes showed. They didn't look like delivery men to Ellen, more like burglars who were hiding stolen goods. But she didn't risk whispering this fear to Mirror-Belle, in case they heard her.

One of the men had opened the shed door and must have been putting the televisions inside, while the other went back through the gate and then reappeared with a large square object covered in a sheet. Probably a stolen picture, thought Ellen.

A sudden idea struck her. If she and Mirror-Belle climbed over the low wall into her own garden, they could get into her house through the back door and phone the police. With a finger over her lips, she pointed at the wall and then beckoned to Mirror-Belle.

Ellen was already over the wall when she realized that Mirror-Belle wasn't following her.

"It's a witch!" she heard one of the men say, and, "Don't be daft, it's a kid," from the other. And then came Mirror-Belle's voice – loud, clear and bossy as ever: "Don't just dump that on the floor. Aren't you going to hang it on the wall?"

Instead of following Ellen, Mirror-Belle must have gone to check what sort of a job the "delivery men" were doing.

Ellen stood frozen, uncertain whether to join Mirror-Belle or run home for help. Then she heard one of the men again. This time he was talking to Mirror-Belle.

"I do apologize, madam. Just step inside and wait while we fetch our tool-box."

The next sounds came quickly. A slam, a metallic clink, some bashing and an angry "Let me out! What is the meaning of this?" from Mirror-Belle. Then footsteps and the creak of the garden gate. The men had locked Mirror-Belle in the shed and escaped!

But *had* they both escaped? Ellen didn't dare investigate by herself. Instead, she ran through her own garden and into the house through the back door.

"Help! Help!" she cried.

Dad came out of the kitchen, followed by Mum and Luke.

"What's the matter? Did a skeleton jump out at you?" Dad asked jokily.

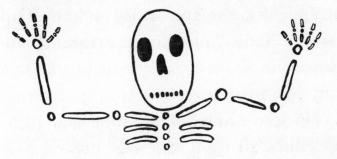

"The burglars have locked Mirror-Belle in the shed next door!" shrieked Ellen. "And now they're getting away!"

Mum and Dad still seemed to think this was some Halloween prank. It was Luke who ran to the front window.

"Two men are getting into a van," he reported. "And they're wearing masks, or hoods, or something."

"Take down the number," said Dad, and reached for the phone to call the police.

Mum made Ellen sit down and drink some hot sweet tea "for shock".

When Ellen protested, "But we must go back next door! Mirror-Belle's trapped! We've got to rescue her!" Dad said, "Not till the police arrive." Ellen knew he thought Mirror-Belle was just an imaginary friend.

"Where's Katy?" said Mum suddenly.

"She's all right. She's at home," said Ellen, but Mum phoned Katy's parents just the same.

"That's strange. She's in bed with a cold," Mum said, sounding relieved but puzzled.

"Yes . . . she couldn't come, but then Mirror-Belle . . ." Ellen began, but a ring at the bell interrupted her explanation. It was the police.

Katy was back at school on Monday. Like the rest of Ellen's class, she had read in the paper about Ellen's discovery of the shed full of stolen goods, and of how the burglars had been caught thanks to Luke getting the number of their van.

"Just think! If only I hadn't had that cold I'd be in the paper too," she said.

"But if you'd come with me instead of Mirror-Belle, we wouldn't have gone to number 17."

"Did the police find Mirror-Belle as well as all the televisions?" asked Katy. Unlike Ellen's family, she believed in Mirror-Belle, who had once come to their school.

"No," said Ellen. "You see, the men hadn't just stolen televisions. When we were there they were hiding away something else. I thought it was a great big picture, but it wasn't."

"What was it, then?" asked Katy.

"It was a mirror," said Ellen.

Chapter Five

The Princess Test

"I hope you haven't put spaghetti on that shopping list," said Ellen to her brother, Luke. "Or mince. Or tinned tomatoes."

"Don't worry, bossyboots, we're not going to have spag bol again." Luke crumpled the shopping list and stuffed it into his pocket. "I'm going to make chicken vindaloo."

"What's that?"

"It's this really hot curry."

Ellen wasn't sure that really hot curry would be the right sort of supper for Mum, who had just had her appendix out. But it was a relief that it wouldn't be yet more spaghetti bolognese, which was what Dad had cooked just about every night of the week Mum had been in hospital. It used to be Ellen's favourite food, but now she didn't mind if she never ate it again.

Mum was coming home today; Dad had gone to fetch her from the hospital. He had warned Ellen and Luke that she would still be a bit weak after the operation and that they would have to be extra helpful. So Luke had agreed to do the shopping and cook the supper, and Ellen was going to make the bedroom look nice for Mum's return.

Luke went out, slamming the front door, and Ellen took the cleaning things upstairs. She had decided to make Mum a "Welcome Home" card and pick some flowers from the garden. But first she really ought to do the boring housework-y things.

She straightened the duvet on the bed and then picked up the yellow duster.

Dust was such funny stuff, she thought to herself. No one actually sprinkled it on the furniture; it just appeared from nowhere. "And what *is* it exactly?" she wondered out loud as she began to dust Mum's dressing table.

"What is what?" came a voice.

"Dust," Ellen replied automatically, and then, "Mirror-Belle! It's you!"

"Yes, though why you should be asking me questions about dust I have no idea. I've never even *seen* dust," said Mirror-Belle in a superior voice.

There were three mirrors on Mum's dressing table: a big one in the middle and, joined on to it, two smaller ones which slanted inwards. Mirror-Belle was

leaning out of
the middle mirror. "You
seem to forget that I'm
a princess, not a maid," she said.

"Oh, no, you're not," came another
voice, and Ellen was amazed to see a second Mirror-Belle – at least, that was
what she looked like – sticking a hand
out of the left-hand mirror and wagging
a finger at the first Mirror-Belle. "You
know very well that you're a maid. You're
my maid." She turned to Ellen and said,

"She's always disguising herself as me. Once, when we were on a journey to another kingdom, she made me swap clothes and horses with her, and when we got there she managed to kid everyone that she was the princess, so I was sent to feed the geese."

"What a pack of lies," said the first Mirror-Belle, who had slithered out of the mirror and was swinging her legs to the ground. "She's got it the wrong way round. *She's* the maid and *I'm* the one who had to feed the geese. But of course my sweet singing soon made everyone realize that I was the real princess."

"You've got a voice like a crow," said the second Mirror-Belle, beginning to slither out herself.

The first one tried to push her back, and Ellen cried, "Be careful or you'll break the glass!"

"Stop this commotion at once!" came another voice. A third identical girl was reaching out from the right-hand mirror and had picked up Mum's silver-backed hairbrush. "Now, you two lazybones, whose turn is it to brush my hair today?"

"Are *you* the real Mirror-Belle?" asked Ellen.

"Naturally – don't you recognize me?" said the newest Mirror-Belle, but the other two said, "Nonsense," and, "She's Ethel, the kitchen maid."

"Well, you all look exactly the same to me," said Ellen. "And none of you looks specially like a princess. You don't really look like maids either. At least, I suppose you have all got dusters, but you haven't got caps and aprons. Really, you all look just like me."

All three Mirror-Belles had a complicated explanation for this, but since they all talked at once Ellen couldn't make out what the different explanations were, and she didn't really care.

"I give up," she said. "In any case, does it really matter who's who?"

"Of course it does!" said all three mirror girls together.

This at least was something they were agreed on.

"I know!" said the first one. "You must give us a test, Ellen, to find out which is the true princess."

"What sort of a test?" Ellen asked.

"Well, if you had a frog, you could see which of us could kiss it and turn it into a prince," said the second girl.

"Or we could lie on the bed and see who could detect if there was a pea under the mattress," suggested the third one. "Only a real princess could do that."

"I haven't got a frog," said Ellen, "and I've only just made the bed. I don't want you all messing it up again." In any case, she had bad memories of pea-detection and frog-kissing. Mirror-Belle had tried these things out in a shop once and got them both into trouble.

Still, Ellen quite liked the idea of a test.

"I'll think of something," she told them. "But first, I must be able to tell you apart. Just stand still a minute."

She took one of Mum's lipsticks from a little drawer in the dressing table. She wrote a big L on the forehead of the Mirror-Belle who had come out of the left mirror. On the foreheads of the other two she wrote R and M, for right and middle.

"What is the test going to be?" they all kept clamouring.

"It's a quiz," said Ellen, "and I'm the quizmaster."

She was enjoying herself. For once she was the one in charge, instead of being ordered about by Mirror-Belle. But it was going to be hard thinking up the questions.

"I'll just put Mum's lipstick back in the drawer," she said, and that made her wonder what a princess would call her own mother. She wouldn't say "Mum", like an ordinary person, surely? But "Your Majesty" didn't sound quite right either. This was something that a real princess would know the answer to, and would make a good quiz question.

"Question number one: what do you call your mother?"

They all answered at once, so Ellen made them take turns.

"Your Mumjesty," said Mirror-Belle L.

"Queen Mother," said Mirror-Belle R.

"O Most Royal Madam whom I Respect and Obey without Question," said Mirror-Belle M.

Ellen couldn't decide which of these sounded right, so she moved on to another question. A dog barking in the distance made her think about Mirror-Belle's dog, Prince Precious Paws, and that gave her another idea.

"What would a real princess give to her dog for his birthday?" she asked.

This time she made them answer in a different order.

"A golden bone," said Mirror-Belle R.

"How common! An emerald-studded collar would be a far more suitable gift," said Mirror-Belle M.

"What's so special about that?" asked Mirror-Belle L. "I'm planning to give Prince Precious Paws something magical – an invisible lead, which will make *him* invisible when I put it on him. In fact, I've brought one for your dog, Splodge, too. Here it is." She reached out to Ellen as if she were handing her something.

The other two Mirror-Belles became very indignant at this.

"She's an impostor!" cried Mirror-Belle R. "Besides, I've brought you a *far* better invisible present. It's . . . um . . . a spoon that will change whatever you're eating into your favourite food."

Ellen didn't really believe in the invisible spoon, but she pretended to take it and said, "I wish I'd had this when Dad was doing the cooking."

"Invisible spoons are two a penny," said Mirror-Belle M scornfully. "I've brought you . . . er . . . some invisible pyjamas. If you wear them at night, all your dreams will come true."

All three Mirror-Belles were crowding round her, offering her more and more invisible things, and Ellen was losing the feeling of being the one in charge. The quiz seemed to have turned into a boasting session.

"And here's an invisible clock . . ." began Mirror-Belle M.

"Stop!" cried Ellen.

The invisible clock had reminded her that Mum would be back from hospital soon. She would never get the bedroom ready at this rate. Not on her own, anyway, and the three Mirror-Belles were so eager to prove that they were not maids they would never agree to help. Unless . . .

Suddenly, Ellen had an idea. "I've thought of a test," she said. "I've just remembered that there is a . . . a sort of fairy imprisoned in the furniture in this room and only a true princess will be able to set her free."

The Mirror-Belles started opening drawers, but Ellen stopped them.

"No, the fairy's not in a drawer or cupboard. She's in the actual *wood* of the furniture. You have to rub the wood to get her out."

"Oh, a wood nymph, you mean," said Mirror-Belle R. "Why didn't you say so before?" and she immediately began to rub the dressing table with her duster.

"She might be in the mantelpiece . . . or in the wood of the bedside table," suggested Ellen, and the other two Mirror-Belles set to work with their dusters.

They were
all rubbing
furiously. Soon
there was not
a speck of
dust to be
seen, and
the furniture
was shiny
bright.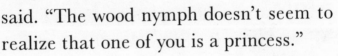

"You've all
failed that
test," Ellen
said. "The wood nymph doesn't seem to
realize that one of you is a princess."

Once again, all three Mirror-Belles
started on explanations for this, but
Ellen interrupted them. "I've thought of
a different test," she said. "Well, it's
more of a quest than a test. Down in the
garden there is a talking flower. But it
will only talk if it's picked and put into a

vase of water by a true princess."

The three girls ran to the bedroom door, eager to be downstairs and out in the garden. Ellen was suddenly afraid that they would pick every single flower, so she called out after them, "The flower will only talk if the princess picks no more than five flowers altogether."

While the Mirror-Belles picked the flowers, Ellen filled a vase with water and put it on Mum's gleaming bedside table. She was just making a start on her "Welcome Home" card when the Mirror-Belles charged back into the room and thrust their flowers into the vase. The flowers looked very pretty but they were completely silent.

"I expect the magic flower is too shy to talk

to me when there are two maids in the room," said one of the Mirror-Belles, and the other two said, "To *me*, you mean."

Just then Ellen heard the front door bang. Help! Was Dad back with Mum already? The room did look really nice now, but how was she going to get rid of the three Mirror-Belles? She was sure Mum wouldn't want them all in her bedroom when she was trying to rest.

"I'm back!" came Luke's voice.

Of course – she should have recognized the way he slammed the door. Still, Mum would be back any minute now.

"Give us another test, Ellen," the Mirror-Belles were demanding, and suddenly Ellen knew what to do.

"All right," she said, "but this one is really difficult. You've given me all these invisible presents, which is very nice of you, but I'm sure that only a real princess would know how to make *herself* invisible."

As Ellen closed her eyes and counted to a hundred, she remembered the very first time she had ever met Mirror-Belle. That time, Mirror-Belle had tricked her by blindfolding her with toilet paper and then disappearing into the bathroom mirror. This time, it was Ellen who was tricking Mirror-Belle. She felt a bit guilty and wondered where she had learned to make up so many stories. But of course she knew the answer really – it was from Mirror-Belle.

As she had hoped, when she got to a hundred and opened her eyes, the room was empty. She was very careful indeed not to steal a glance at the mirrors on the dressing table, in case the mirror princesses (or maids) reappeared. Instead, she lay on her tummy on the floor and carried on with the "Welcome Home" card.

She had just finished it when she heard the front door opening again.

Ellen jumped to her feet and ran downstairs into the arms of the person she most wanted to see in the whole world.

"Come and look at your bedroom, Mum!" she said.

"Don't tire her out," said Dad, but Mum laughed and let herself be tugged upstairs by Ellen.

She admired the card and the flowers and the neatly made bed. "And what shining surfaces!" she said. "I never knew you were so good at housework, Ellen! It's a real treat to come home to this."

Ellen wished that Mirror-Belle could hear. She was the one who deserved most of the praise.

"I wanted you to have a nice treat to come home to," she muttered to Mum.

Mum hugged her again and said, "Do you know what the biggest treat is? Seeing you!"

A strong spicy smell was wafting into the room.

"That smells even better than spaghetti bolognese," said Mum, and together they went downstairs.

Princess
MIRROR-BELLE
and the Flying Horse

For Alyssa

Contents

✳

✳

✳

✳

✳

Chapter One

The Flying Horse

"There!" said the nurse with the blue belt, looking proudly at the hard white plaster on Ellen's right arm. "All ready for your friends to write their names on it."

Ellen had fallen off her bike and broken her arm, and Mum had taken her to hospital. The arm wasn't hurting nearly as much as it had at first, and Ellen liked the idea of her friends writing their names on the plaster.

"Can I go back to school tomorrow?" she asked eagerly.

"No," said the nurse. "The doctor

wants you to stay in hospital tonight, just so we can keep an eye on you. It's because you had concussion."

"What's that?"

"It's when you bang your head and forget things."

It was true that Ellen's head had hit the pavement when she fell off her bike, and for a minute or so she hadn't been able to remember where she was or what had happened.

"I'm always telling her to wear her cycle helmet," said Mum to the nurse.

Ellen looked at the floor and felt guilty. "Sorry," she muttered. "But I feel fine now."

"All the same, we need to keep you in to be on the safe side." The nurse turned to Mum and added, "I expect you'll be able to take her home tomorrow, after the doctor's done his ward round."

A porter appeared with a wheelchair. "Sit in this, old lady," he said to Ellen, and, "You'll have to walk, young lady," to Mum.

It seemed strange to Ellen that she should need a wheelchair when it was her arm and not her leg that she had broken, but she was too shy to say so. The porter wheeled her in and out of a lift and then along a corridor into a room with six beds in it.

"This is Jupiter Ward," he said. "You'll get five-star treatment in here." He parked the wheelchair at the reception desk.

A nurse with a red belt welcomed Ellen and Mum. "I'm Sister Jo," she told them. She showed Ellen her bed, which had a curtain you could draw all round it. Then she fitted a plastic bracelet on to Ellen's left wrist. It had her name on it.

"You'll need to put these on too." Sister Jo was holding out some hospital pyjamas.

"But how will I get the top on over the plaster?" Ellen asked.

"Don't worry — we think of everything," said Sister Jo. When Mum helped Ellen put the pyjamas on they found that the right sleeve had been cut off and the armhole widened so that the plaster could fit through it.

"I'd better go back home now," said Mum.

Ellen felt a bit scared. "I don't want you to go," she said.

"You'll be fine. It's only for one night. And I'm sure you'll make friends with the other children."

But looking around Jupiter Ward, Ellen could see only one other child, a boy who was asleep. Three of the beds were empty and the other one had its curtains drawn around it.

"Hardly anyone seems to be breaking any bones these days," said Sister Jo. "If it wasn't for you, Ellen, I might lose my job!"

Ellen smiled, and found she felt less scared. She hugged Mum goodbye with her left arm and made her promise to bring in a bunch of grapes and a library book the next day.

"Now, down to business," said Sister Jo when Mum had gone. "You need to choose what you want to eat tomorrow. Are you left-handed by any chance?"

"No," said Ellen, puzzled. "Do you do different meals for left-handed people then?"

Sister Jo laughed. "No – but it might be a bit difficult

for you to fill this in." She showed Ellen a yellow card with some writing on it. "It's got the different food choices for breakfast and lunch," she said.

Ellen chose cornflakes and orange juice for breakfast, and chicken pie and fruit salad for lunch. Sister Jo ticked the boxes for her.

"I'm going off duty now," she said. "I'll be back tomorrow lunchtime, but you might be gone by then."

Ellen was sorry to see Sister Jo go. Another nurse took her temperature, and then a different one brought her some cocoa and yet another one took her to the bathroom. It was bewildering having so many different people to look after her and Ellen suddenly felt tired. One of the nurses tucked her up in her new bed.

"Just ring this bell if you want anything in the night," she said.

*

Ellen was woken by a light tap on her shoulder. At first she thought it was Mum, but then she opened her eyes, saw the nurse and remembered where she was. Although she hadn't felt ill enough to ring the bell, it hadn't been a good night. Because of the plaster she couldn't sleep on her right side like she usually did, and it was hard to find a comfortable position. Then she had been woken up very early to have her temperature taken, after which she had fallen into a much deeper sleep.

"We couldn't wake you up when the breakfast trolley came round," the nurse said now. "But don't worry – we've saved yours for you. You should have time to eat it before Doctor Birch comes."

"Have I got time to go to the bathroom too?" asked Ellen.

"Yes. Do you want someone to come and help you?"

"No, thanks." But once Ellen was in the bathroom she found it was quite awkward washing and cleaning her teeth with only her left hand.

"I'll have to learn to write left-handed too," she said aloud.

"That's a good idea," came a voice from the bathroom mirror. "Who knows? That way you might start doing the letters the right way round at last."

Ellen knew that voice very well. It belonged to Princess Mirror-Belle.

Princess Mirror-Belle looked just like Ellen's reflection, but whereas most reflections stay in the mirror, Mirror-Belle had a habit of coming out of it. Although she looked like Ellen, she was not at all like her in character. Ellen was quite shy, but Mirror-Belle was extremely boastful and was full of stories about the palace and the fairy-tale land she said she came from.

Mirror-Belle was dressed in hospital pyjamas just like Ellen, but her plaster was on her left arm.

"Well, don't just stand there staring," she said. "I'll need a bit of help getting out of here." She stuck her right arm out of the mirror and added, "Don't pull too hard. I don't want to break this one as well."

Although Ellen wasn't really sure that she wanted Mirror-Belle in hospital with her, it seemed too late to change things, so she grasped her hand and helped her to wriggle out on to the washbasin and down to the floor. "Did you fall off your bike too?" she asked.

"Certainly not," replied Mirror-Belle. "Would you expect a princess to ride around on anything as common as a bicycle? No . . ." She hesitated for a second and then went on, "I fell off my flying horse."

"You never told me you had a flying horse."

"Well, I'm sorry, Ellen, but I can't tell you all the things I have. It would take too long and it would just make you jealous."

"Were you wearing a riding hat?" asked Ellen. But Mirror-Belle wasn't listening. She had opened the bathroom door and was sauntering into Jupiter Ward.

Ellen was about to follow her, but then

decided to hang back. Somehow she couldn't face trying to explain to the nurses about Mirror-Belle.

She peeped out of the bathroom door and saw her mirror friend climbing into her own bed and ringing the bell above it.

One of the nurses came scurrying to her bedside.

"What is this food supposed to be?" Mirror-Belle asked, pointing to the breakfast tray on the table beside her bed.

"It's what you ordered. Cornflakes and orange juice."

"Cornflakes? What are they? Take them away and bring me a lightly boiled peacock's egg."

The nurse tittered. She seemed to think this was a joke.

"Don't laugh when I'm giving you your orders," said Mirror-Belle. "It's very rude. You can take the orange juice away too. I'd rather have a glass of fresh morning dew with ice and lemon."

"You're not getting anything else," said the nurse. "Anway, the breakfast trolley's gone now."

"Then call it back again this second."

The nurse picked up the untouched breakfast tray and scurried off with it, nearly bumping into a man in a white coat with a stethoscope round his neck. Ellen guessed that he must be Dr Birch.

"I think she's taken a turn for the worse," murmured the nurse with the tray.

The doctor went over to the bed and drew the curtains round it. Ellen, still peeping out of the bathroom, couldn't see him any longer, but she heard his voice.

"It's Ellen, isn't it?" the doctor was saying.

"No, it's Princess Mirror-Belle. I hope you're properly trained to look after royalty. That stethoscope looks very ordinary. The palace doctor has one made of silver and snakeskin."

Dr Birch chuckled. "My little niece likes playing princesses too," he said. "Very well, Your Royal Highness. Now, I want you to tell me everything you can remember about your accident. I see from your notes that you fell off your bike."

"Then your notes are wrong," said Mirror-Belle. "I fell off my flying horse. I'm a very good rider, actually, so I can't quite think how it happened. I suspect that my wicked fairy godmother was up to her tricks again – loosening the saddle or something."

"So you have no memory of any bike

ride? Maybe that's because you banged
your head on the pavement."

"I did no such thing!" said Mirror-
Belle indignantly. "There aren't any
pavements where I live. I landed . . .
um . . . in a stork's nest on the palace
roof. Luckily there weren't any stork's
eggs in it at the time, otherwise—"

"Just a minute!" interrupted the doctor. His voice sounded quite different

suddenly – urgent and excited. "It says here that you broke your right arm."

"I do wish you'd stop reading those stupid notes and listen to me instead," complained Mirror-Belle.

"It's not just the notes. The   -ray shows it quite clearly too. The right arm was broken, but they've plastered the left one!"

"It sounds as if you should sack the plasterer as well as the note-taker."

"How does your right arm feel? Does it still hurt?"

"Now you mention it, it is a little sore. I think that must be from where the storks pecked it. They didn't realize who I was, you see. They probably thought I was a cuckoo who was about to lay its egg in their nest."

Doctor Birch obviously wasn't interested in storks or cuckoos, because Ellen saw him emerge from behind the curtains, almost run to the reception desk and pick up the telephone. His back was turned and Ellen could only catch a few words, such as "mistake", "urgent" and "emergency". She guessed that he was speaking to someone in the plaster room.

This had gone too far, Ellen decided. She really ought to explain everything to the doctor and nurses. She was just braving herself to stride out from the bathroom when she saw someone famil-iar come into Jupiter Ward. It was the same porter who had wheeled her there yesterday, and he was pushing an empty wheelchair.

"You again, old lady?" she heard him say to Mirror-Belle.

Ellen didn't think Mirror-Belle would like being called "old lady" and expected her to tell the nice porter off, but instead Mirror-Belle answered, "Ah – at least someone recognizes that I'm not just an

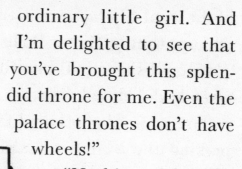

ordinary little girl. And I'm delighted to see that you've brought this splendid throne for me. Even the palace thrones don't have wheels!"

"Nothing but the best for you, old lady," said the porter, and he wheeled her out of Jupiter Ward.

Oh dear! Ellen had to stop this. If Mirror-Belle's left arm really was broken, it wouldn't do for the plaster to be taken off.

Maybe the easiest person to explain things to would be the nice porter. Ellen stepped out of the bathroom and glanced around the ward. The doctor was talking to the nurse at the reception desk. They were gazing deeply into each other's eyes and didn't notice Ellen as she slipped out of the ward. She was just in time to see the porter pushing Mirror-Belle into a lift.

"Stop!" she cried, but the doors had already slid closed.

There was another lift and Ellen pressed the button to call it. It took a long time to come, but at least it was empty when it arrived, so no one could give her funny looks or ask what she was doing on her own.

If the plaster room was where her own arm had been plastered, Ellen was pretty sure it was on the ground floor, so she pressed the G button. But when the lift stopped and she got out, there was no sign of Mirror-Belle or the porter. Ellen found herself in a long corridor with lots of doors leading off it. She looked at the notices on some of the doors but they weren't much help because she couldn't understand what the words meant: one said "Endocrinology", another said

"Haematology" and a third "Toxicology". Ellen was just wondering whether one of these "ology" words was a special medical way of writing "plaster room" when the Haematology door swung open and a nurse with a purple belt came out.

"Can I help you?" she asked Ellen. She looked and sounded quite kind.

"I'm looking for the plaster room," said Ellen.

"Isn't anyone with you? Where have you come from?"

Ellen hesitated, wondering what to tell the nurse. She decided on the truth, even though she doubted if she would be believed.

"I've come from Jupiter Ward," she said, "but they don't know I'm here. You see, they thought my friend Princess Mirror-Belle was me. The thing is, Mirror-Belle broke her left arm but—"

"Just a minute," Purple Belt interrupted her. "Perhaps I'd better phone Jupiter Ward and see what's going on." She took Ellen to an office with a phone in it.

"I think I've got a patient of yours here." Purple Belt took Ellen's left hand and read the identity bracelet round her wrist. "She's called Ellen Page, and she says she's supposed to be in the plaster room . . . That's all right then; I just wanted to check, because she seems a bit confused . . . talking about princesses and things like that . . . oh, I see – concussion; yes, that would fit . . . No, it's OK, I can take her there myself.".

Purple Belt put down the phone and ↕ed brightly at Ellen. "They offered to send another porter, but it's only just round the corner," she said. She took Ellen to a door with a couple of chairs outside it.

Ellen knew she was in the right place because she could hear a familiar voice from inside the room: "My horse's name is Little Lord Lightning. Unfortunately he's been suffering from wing-ache recently. I really ought to take him to the palace vet."

Purple Belt smiled at Ellen and rolled her eyes. "You might have a bit of a wait. It sounds as if there's quite a difficult patient in there."

Ellen decided against saying, "It's Princess Mirror-Belle." Purple Belt would just think she was still confused. Instead she answered, "I don't mind waiting."

"Goodbye then," said Purple Belt. "You won't wander off, will you?"

"No," promised Ellen, sitting down on one of the chairs. She watched Purple Belt disappear down the corridor. Now that she had tracked Mirror-Belle down she found she was dreading the idea of barging into the plaster room and explaining everything to the nurse in there.

"That's funny," came a voice from the room, interrupting Mirror-Belle's account of her flying horse. "I can't read the name on your bracelet. The letters look kind of back to front. I'd better go and get my reading glasses – they're in my coat pocket." A nurse came out of the room. It wasn't the same one who had put Ellen's arm in plaster, though she had a blue belt like hers.

The nurse hurried down the corridor and Ellen, relieved at this chance to talk to Mirror-Belle on her own, slipped into the room.

Mirror-Belle was standing by the window, holding a large pair of scissors in her right hand. "Oh, hello, Ellen," she said. "Do you think these scissors are really suitable for cutting a royal plaster? They look rather poor quality to me. I thought I might try them out on a few things myself before the servant returns." She aimed the scissors at the curtains.

"Stop!" cried Ellen. She grabbed the scissors from Mirror-Belle. "The nurse will be back in a second and you've got to go!" she told her.

"Don't you start ordering me around, Ellen," Mirror-Belle reproached her.

"You're getting to be as bad as your servants. I'll come and go as I please."

"But surely you don't want to stay and have your plaster cut off? If you've broken your arm, you need it."

"Good point," said Mirror-Belle. "Now you're talking sense. Perhaps I should go back and see how Little Lord Lightning is getting on. Besides, no one here seems to have any respect for royalty – except for the throne-pusher, that is. He was extremely polite. I might see if I can find a job for him in the palace."

"Mirror-Belle, just go – please!" Ellen begged.

"All in good time," replied Mirror-Belle. She picked up a pen from a table.

"What are you doing now?" Ellen felt rattled. Everything would be so much easier if Mirror-Belle had gone by the time Blue Belt came back.

In reply, Mirror-Belle held the pen

out to her. "As a special honour, I'm going to allow you to be the first person to sign my plaster," she said.

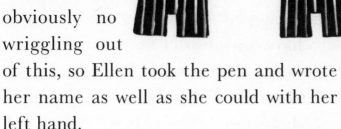

There was obviously no wriggling out of this, so Ellen took the pen and wrote her name as well as she could with her left hand.

"Really, Ellen, this is even worse than your normal writing. As well as being backwards, the letters are awfully wobbly."

"They're not backwards – and they only look wobbly because I'm writing left-handed."

"I'll show you how it should be done," said Mirror-Belle, taking the pen from

Ellen. She wrote her own name on Ellen's plaster. It looked like this:

Mirror-Belle

"Talk about backwards and wobbly," Ellen couldn't help muttering, even though there wasn't time for an argument. She glanced round the room, hoping to see a mirror, but there was none.

Just then they heard footsteps in the corridor. Blue Belt was coming back!

"Farewell!" cried Mirror-Belle, and she darted out of the door. Ellen peered out and saw her go through a door on the other side of the corridor. It had another of the long "ology" words written on it. "Ophthalmology," this one said.

"Now, now," said Blue Belt, coming into the plaster room. "You were supposed to stay sitting down. It's funny," she added, "I thought for a moment that

I saw you going into the eye department, but it must have been someone else."

She put on her reading glasses and looked at Ellen's identity bracelet.

"That's good – I can read it fine now," she said. "Ellen Page." She checked the name against Ellen's notes, and then frowned. "There's no problem with the name, but I can't understand what the doctor's written. It says, 'Remove plaster from left arm and plaster right arm,' but your right arm *is* plastered. I suppose he must mean, 'Remove plaster from right arm and plaster left arm'."

"No, no!" exclaimed Ellen in alarm. "It's the right one that's broken. The left one works fine." She waved it about to prove her point.

Blue Belt checked the notes and the -ray. "Well, it's all very strange," she said. "I do wonder if that Doctor Birch's mind is always on his work."

She phoned for a porter to take Ellen back to Jupiter Ward and then frowned again. "It's funny," she said, "but I could have sworn the plaster was on your left arm too! Before I fetched my glasses, that is. I really ought to pop into the eye department and get my sight checked."

At that moment there was a babble of voices in the corridor and someone knocked on the door. Blue Belt opened it, and Ellen heard three voices speaking at once. As far as she could make out, a woman was asking, "Is she in here?" and a boy was saying, "I keep telling you what happened," and a man was saying, "Be quiet, Toby."

"I'm sorry – who are you looking for?" asked Blue Belt.

"I don't even know her name, but I thought she might have been one of your patients," came the woman's voice. "I was just checking little Toby's eyesight –

you know, that test where they have to read the letters in the mirror – and this girl with her arm in plaster came charging in. She was talking a lot of nonsense, something about all the letters being back to front. She refused to leave when I asked her to, so I went to get the doctor to help me, but when we got back she'd just disappeared."

"Yes – into the mirror!" came the boy's voice.

"Don't be silly, Toby. You know that's impossible," said the man.

"But I saw her!"

"Yes, but don't forget you need new glasses."

"Well, I'm sorry," said Blue Belt, "but whoever she is, she's not in here."

Ellen had found a blanket and covered herself with it, terrified that the people outside would come in, see her and accuse her of Mirror-Belle's bad behaviour. But they seemed happy to accept what Blue Belt said, and she heard the woman saying, "Maybe she belongs on Jupiter Ward. I'll try phoning them."

Blue Belt shook her head when they had gone. "Everybody seems to be going mad today," she said. "Except you, Charlie," she added to the nice porter who had just come into the room.

"Hello, old lady – has that naughty nurse been drawing pictures on your plaster?" he said to Ellen. Ellen smiled faintly and sat down in the wheelchair.

"You've gone all quiet," he told her as he pushed her into the lift. "Aren't you going to tell me any more stories about your flying horse?" Ellen just shook her head and closed her eyes. She suddenly felt very tired.

Back in Jupiter Ward, two friendly people were there to greet her – Sister Jo and Mum. Mum was looking quite worried. "I hear you've been a bit delirious," she said.

"No, I'm fine," said Ellen.

"If you ask me," said Sister Jo in a low voice, "it's that Doctor Birch who's been a bit delirious. Fancy not knowing his right from his left! I think he must be in love. I'm going to ask Doctor Hamza to see you as soon as you've had your lunch. You must be starving – I gather you didn't fancy your breakfast."

"That's not like you, Ellen," said Mum.

Ellen, who didn't feel like explaining, gobbled up her chicken pie and fruit salad. She was halfway through the bunch of grapes that Mum had brought

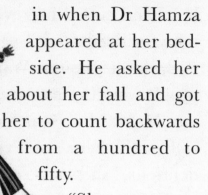

in when Dr Hamza appeared at her bedside. He asked her about her fall and got her to count backwards from a hundred to fifty.

"She seems very fine and dandy to me," he told Mum. "You can take her home."

Mum had brought in some new clothes, including a blouse with a cut-off sleeve like the hospital pyjama top. She helped Ellen into them.

"Do you want to pop into the bathroom before you go?" asked Sister Jo. "Then you can see in the mirror how smart you look."

"No!" said Ellen. "I mean, no, thank you. Can I go back to school now and show everyone the plaster?"

"That can wait till tomorrow," said Mum. "I think you should take things easy this afternoon. You can finish the grapes and read the new library book I've got out for you."

"What's it called?" asked Ellen.

"*The Flying Horse*," said Mum, and couldn't understand why Ellen laughed all the way down in the lift.

Chapter Two

The Magic Ball

"Don't get too many yellow cards, Ellen!" said Dad.

Ellen's big brother Luke chortled at this, but Ellen just smiled thinly. "I might not even play football," she said. "There are lots of other sports you can choose."

The leisure centre was having an open day. Dad and Luke were going to play a game of squash, and Ellen was doing something called "Four for Free", which meant you could try out four sports without paying anything.

"We'll be on squash court three," said

Dad. "Just in case you need me to sort out any refs for you!" he added.

Luke chuckled again. "I think I'd better do that, Dad. You won't be in a fit state after I've beaten you!" Then the two of them strode off, swinging their rackets jauntily.

Ellen decided to try out the Eight and Over gym first. It didn't have any weight-lifting machines like the big gym, but it did have a trampoline and some running and cycling machines.

She showed her Four for Free card to the muscular young attendant in the gym. He ticked one of the boxes on it and handed it back to her.

The gym was very busy but Ellen found a free running machine. She'd never been on one before so the attendant had to show her how to use it.

It felt strange at first to run on the spot. Ellen was just getting the hang of it when she heard a voice saying, "You're going the wrong way!"

Ellen had been concentrating so hard on her feet and the little screen showing her speed that she had hardly taken in the row of mirrors facing the running machines. Startled 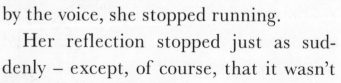 by the voice, she stopped running.

Her reflection stopped just as suddenly – except, of course, that it wasn't really her reflection; it was Princess Mirror-Belle.

"Mirror-Belle! What are you doing here?" asked Ellen.

Princess Mirror-Belle jumped off her machine and jogged out of the mirror and into the gym. "Chasing the magic ball," she said. "Have you seen it?"

Ellen looked round. She couldn't see a ball, and she was relieved that no one else in the gym seemed to have noticed Mirror-Belle; they were all too busy bouncing and running or cycling.

"What magic ball?" she asked.

"The one my wicked fairy godmother threw," said Mirror-Belle. "She's been up to her tricks again. She's turned everyone in the palace to stone."

"Except for you," remarked Ellen.

"Yes, well, she was going to do it to me too, but luckily I knew the special magic words to stop her."

"What were they?"

Mirror-Belle looked rather annoyed, and said, "Don't hold me up – I told you, I have to find the magic ball."

"You still haven't explained about that," said Ellen.

"Haven't I? Well, the wicked fairy threw it and said that the stone spell would only be broken if I could bring it back to her. You should have heard her cackle!"

"Why was she cackling?"

"Because everyone knows that it's almost impossible to keep up with her magic ball. I've been chasing it for days – through forests and up and down mountains – but it's always just ahead of me. And now I seem to have lost sight of it altogether."

Mirror-Belle glanced round the gym and then her eyes lit up. "Aha!" she said, and she marched up to the muscular attendant.

"You can't fool me," she told him, and she jumped up and tapped his arm.

"Stop mucking about," he said.

"That's no way to talk to a princess," said Mirror-Belle. "And, in any case, you're the one who's mucking about. Roll up your sleeve immediately!"

"Stop it, Mirror-Belle," said Ellen. "You'll get us chucked out."

"But it's perfectly clear he's hiding the magic ball up his sleeve," said Mirror-Belle.

"Don't be silly – that's not a ball, it's just his arm muscles," said Ellen, laughing.

The attendant looked quite amused and actually did roll up his right sleeve. He was probably glad to have a chance to display his bulging biceps.

Mirror-Belle looked unimpressed and demanded to see the other arm. But by now the attendant had had enough.

Perhaps he thought they were trying to make fun of him.

"Why don't you two buzz off and try out something else," he said. Then a suspicious look crossed his face. "Have I ticked both your cards?" he asked.

Ellen showed him hers, and Mirror-Belle also took a card from the pocket of her tracksuit trousers. The attendant stared at it. "That's funny," he said. "The writing's all wrong on this one."

Ellen glanced at Mirror-Belle's card. She was not surprised to see that it was in mirror-writing. Instead of saying FOUR FOR FREE it said:

ƎƎᴚ Ꭱ⊖Ⅎ ᴚꓴ⊖Ⅎ

"It's perfectly correct," said Mirror-Belle. "You probably just left school too young, before you'd fully mastered the art of reading." She shook her head and turned to Ellen. "All muscles and no brain," she murmured. Ellen couldn't help giggling.

The attendant was really cross now. "Get out!" he said.

Ellen tugged at Mirror-Belle's arm. "Why don't we have a go at five-a-side football?" she said.

"Football, did you say? That sounds promising!"

To Ellen's relief, Mirror-Belle seemed to forget about the muscular attendant's left arm and she followed Ellen out of the gym and down the stairs.

In the five-a-side hall a woman in a pink tracksuit looked pleased to see them.

"Good – we needed an extra two to get started," she said. "I hope you don't mind being on different teams." After hurriedly checking their cards, she gave Ellen a blue armband and Mirror-Belle a red one and told them where to stand. Then she put a football down in the middle of the pitch.

Mirror-Belle looked disappointed. "That's not the magic ball," she said. "It's too big, and it's the wrong colour. I'll have to search elsewhere."

"Oh, do stay," said Ellen. "Otherwise your team will be one short."

Mirror-Belle shrugged her shoulders. Pink Tracksuit blew a whistle, and everyone started running around, kicking the ball and trying to score goals.

One of the other children on the red team passed the ball to Mirror-Belle and she picked it up. "Thank you," she said, "but it's no use to me. Here, Ellen, catch!" And ignoring Pink Tracksuit, who was blowing her whistle, she threw the ball to Ellen.

The others on the red team started shouting at Mirror-Belle.

"Stupid!"

"You're not allowed to use your hands."

"She's on the other side anyway."

Mirror-Belle looked shocked. She went up to Pink Tracksuit. "Excuse me – you seem to be in charge. What is the punishment for being rude to royalty? In my father's kingdom these people would have to weed the palace gardens for a year."

Pink Tracksuit ignored this. "Free kick for the blues," she announced and, "Get back in your place," she told Mirror-Belle.

"Just who do you think you are?" Mirror-Belle asked her.

"I'm the coach," said Pink Tracksuit.

Mirror-Belle started to laugh. "In that case, where are your six white horses?

Where are your wheels and your velvet cushions? Where are the driver and the footmen?"

Pink Tracksuit looked as if she might send Mirror-Belle off, and Ellen tried to come to the rescue. "I'm sorry," she said. "I don't think she's ever played football before." She managed to coax Mirror-Belle back on to the pitch. "You have to kick the ball, and only to people in your team – or into the goal," she told her. "That's the net thing," she added, point- ing, as Mirror-Belle was looking blank.

Pink Tracksuit blew the whistle and the game started up again. The blue team scored a goal, and then another one. Then the reds got the ball. One of them passed it to Mirror-Belle.

"No – not to her," moaned another red player, but it was too late. Mirror-Belle had given the ball a huge kick. It landed in the red team's goal.

"Yes!" shouted some of the blues, jumping up and down, but the reds were furious.

"You idiot!"

"That was an own goal!"

"Get her off!"

Once again Mirror-Belle strode up to Pink Tracksuit. "I'm simply not putting up with this petty jealousy," she complained.

"We're not jealous!" said one of the reds.

"Yes, you are. I've just done what those two other people did – kicked the ball into the net – but, if I may say so, with far greater skill and style than they did. I can't help it if the rest of you can't match up to me."

"But it was the wrong goal! You should have kicked it into the blue goal!"

"Really," said Mirror-Belle, "I can't be bothered with all these silly details. You'll just have to play four-a-side. Come on, Ellen, let's go."

Ellen thought this was a good idea, and so did everyone else.

"Well, that was a waste of time," said Mirror-Belle as they left the football hall. "Now maybe I'll never find the magic ball, and my parents and all the servants will remain statues for ever. I suppose in that case I'd have to come and live with you, Ellen."

Ellen wasn't too sure about this plan. A little of Mirror-Belle went a long way. Luckily she was saved from replying because Mirror-Belle stopped suddenly outside a door and said, "Just a minute, do I hear bouncing? What's in there?"

"It's the indoor tennis courts." Tennis was one of the sports you could choose as part of Four for Free, although after the football experience Ellen wasn't keen for Mirror-Belle to join in.

But she had no choice. Mirror-Belle had already opened the door, and a jolly-looking woman in white shorts and a T-shirt was greeting them.

"Hi there, four-for-frees! Jolly good – now we can play doubles; what fun!" She gave them both tennis rackets and introduced them to two other girls called Jade and Ailsa. Then she asked Ellen, "Do you two want to play together or opposite each other?"

"Together," said Ellen hastily, remembering the disastrous football game.

A lot of yellow tennis balls were lying on the ground and Mirror-Belle was inspecting them. "These are the right colour, but they're too furry, and they're not trying to escape," she said.

The jolly woman laughed heartily. "Now, how about a little knockabout before you start a proper game?" she suggested. "You serve first, Mirror-Belle."

"Naturally," said Mirror-Belle. She picked up a ball and hit it to Ellen.

Jade and Ailsa giggled, and the jolly woman said, "Whoopsadaisy!"

"You're not supposed to pass it to me," said Ellen.

"Why ever not? You're on my team, aren't you?"

"Yes."

"Well, in that other stupid game you said I was to pass the ball to people on the same team. Which is it to be? Do make up your mind – I haven't got all day."

"Well, you see . . ." Ellen was about to explain the difference between football and tennis when Mirror-Belle's face lit up. "Oh, I understand!" she said, and picked up the ball. This time it hit the net. "Goal!" she cried.

Jade and Ailsa giggled some more, but the jolly woman said, "Don't laugh at her. She's doing her best." Then she turned to Mirror-Belle. "Try hitting it a little higher and you'll get it over all right."

"But surely it wouldn't be a goal if it went over the net?" said Mirror-Belle.

"You don't score goals in tennis," Ellen told her. "You have to keep hitting the ball over the net till the other side can't manage to hit it back."

"Well really, this is too tiresome for words. Things are so much simpler back home. When I play with my own golden ball I just throw it and catch it – there's none of this nonsense about teams and goals and nets and red and blue. Occasionally, of course, the ball falls into a pond, but then it usually gets rescued by a frog and I turn him into a prince by kissing him."

The jolly woman laughed again, more uncertainly this time. "I tell you what," she said. "I think you two would enjoy putting. That's quite a straightforward game."

"That's a good idea," said Ellen, but only as a way of getting out of the embarrassing tennis game. She didn't really want to try another sport with Mirror-

Belle, and once they were outside in the corridor she said, "Maybe the magic ball has bounced back to your land, Mirror-Belle. Don't you think you ought to go back and look for it there?"

"No, I'm sure it's here somewhere." They had reached the reception area and Mirror-Belle looked around. "What about this butting game? Is there a ball in that?"

"It's putting, not butting," said Ellen, alarmed by the thought of Mirror-Belle trying to head-butt a golf ball. "Yes, there is a ball, but . . . "

A receptionist overheard them. "Do you want the putting green? Go out through the main door and turn left," she said, and the next second Mirror-Belle was prancing eagerly outside. Ellen followed her doubtfully.

The attendant on the putting green gave them each a club and a ball. Ellen was relieved to find that they could play by themselves, without having to join another group of children.

Mirror-Belle looked disappointed with her ball. "There's nothing magic about this," she said, but she was intrigued by the metal flags sticking out of the ground, each one with a number on it.

"How curious," she said. "At home we fly the flag of the kingdom high above the palace. It has a lion and a unicorn on it – except that by now I suppose the wicked fairy must have taken it down and replaced it with her own horrible flag."

"What's that got on it?" asked Ellen.

"Er . . . a spider and a centipede," replied

Mirror-Belle. "Still, even that's a bit better than these silly flags in the ground."

"But these ones are different. They're just for the game – to show you where the holes are," Ellen tried to explain.

Instead of listening to her, Mirror-Belle was swinging her golf club about experimentally, as if it was a tennis racket.

"No, not like that. You have to put the ball on the ground, then hit it."

"Get a move on, can't you," came a voice from behind them, and Ellen saw that three boys were queuing up to have a game.

Feeling flustered, she said to Mirror-Belle, "Why don't I go first, so I can show you? I'm not very good, mind."

She stood with her feet apart, swung her club back and gave the ball a smart tap. To her surprise it ended up really near the hole. With a bit of luck she should get it in with the next shot. Ellen felt quite pleased with herself and hoped that the impatient boys were impressed.

But what was Mirror-Belle up to? Instead of placing her own ball on the ground she was running after Ellen's one. And now she was whacking it back in Ellen's direction – except that it went sailing past her and hit one of the impatient boys.

"What do you think you're doing?" he yelled, clutching his knee.

"Returning the ball, of course," said Mirror-Belle. "And it was a pretty good shot, if you ask me. Ellen here didn't manage to get it back – that's one point to me."

"No, it's not!" Ellen found herself shouting at Mirror-Belle. "I wish you'd listen to me. This isn't tennis, it's putting. It's like golf – you have to get the ball down the hole."

"Well, really!" Mirror-Belle too sounded loud and indignant. "I must say, I thought better of you, Ellen. You keep making me play these stupid games when you know I should be looking for the magic ball, and then you change all the rules to suit yourself."

"No, I don't. And I don't want you to play with me anyway. It was your idea."

"I thought you were my friend," said Mirror-Belle. For the first time ever, Ellen thought she could see tears in her eyes. But she couldn't be sure because the next second Mirror-Belle had thrown down her club and was running away, back towards the main doors of the leisure centre.

"What a nutcase," said the boy with the hurt knee. One of the others seemed to feel sorry for Ellen. "You can play with us if you like," he offered.

"No, it's all right. I'd better make it up with her."

Ellen returned the clubs and balls to the attendant and then followed in Mirror-Belle's footsteps.

"Have you seen my friend?" she asked the receptionist.

"Oh, I thought she was your twin. Yes, she was here a minute ago. She looked a bit upset. She went into the crèche."

Ellen's heart sank. The crèche was only supposed to be for toddlers and very young children; they could stay there and be looked after while their parents played sports or went to the gym. What on earth was Mirror-Belle up to in there?

She found out as soon as she opened the door and a lightweight blue ball hit her, followed by a red one.

Mirror-Belle was in the ball pool, hurling the balls out of it at a frantic speed. A few excited toddlers were copying her and some others were running around outside the ball pool, picking up the balls and throwing them around. Everyone seemed to be having a good time except for the two women in charge of the crèche. One of them was telling Mirror-Belle off; the other one, seeing Ellen coming in, looked up from the nappy she was changing and said,

"Is that girl in the ball pool your twin? Can you tell her to stop throwing the balls around?"

"She's not, but I'll try," said Ellen and went up to the ball pool.

"Ah, Ellen, there you are at last!" Mirror-Belle greeted her in a friendly voice.

She seemed to have forgotten about their quarrel. "Do you know, that wicked fairy is even more cunning than I thought. She's obviously sent the magic ball in here and she thinks I won't be able to find it among all the others. But I'm sure I'll recognize it. For a start, a lot of them are the wrong colour." She threw a green ball out. "And so far none of the yellow ones feel right. They don't bounce properly." She hurled a couple of yellow balls in different directions. One of them landed softly on the tummy of the baby whose nappy was being changed. He clutched it and burbled happily.

"I expect the magic ball has sunk to the bottom," went on Mirror-Belle. "I'll probably have to get rid of all the others before I find it."

"Mirror-Belle, you've got to stop that! You're not supposed to be in here anyway."

"Who said so? I don't notice any kings or queens around here and they are the only ones who can tell princesses what to do or where to go," said Mirror-Belle.

"But you're too old for the crèche," said Ellen.

"In any case, you have to be signed in by your mother or father," added one of the crèche-workers. She was wearing a badge with a smiley face and the name Tracy on it.

Mirror-Belle looked at her as if she was an idiot. "That's impossible," she said. "As I've already told you, both my parents have been turned to stone."

"Fwo! Fwo! Fwo!" shouted a toddler, eager for some more action. He clamped his arms round one of Mirror-Belle's legs. Obligingly, Mirror-Belle threw a few more balls out of the pool.

Tracy turned to Ellen, hoping to get

more sense out of her. "Where are your parents?" she asked.

"Well, my dad's on squash court three," Ellen admitted. "But he's not *her* father," she added hastily.

"Fwo! Fwo!" the toddler started to clamour again, but Mirror-Belle ignored him. "You never told me your father had a court like mine," she said to Ellen in surprise. "How many courtiers does he have waiting on him?"

"It's not that sort of court – not a royal one," said Ellen. "Dad's playing squash with Luke."

"Oh," said Mirror-Belle, appearing to lose interest. She threw a few more balls around, but rather half-heartedly. Then, all of a sudden, she unclamped the demanding toddler from her leg and sprang out of the ball pool. "I think I've been on the wrong trail all the time," she announced. She ran to the door, flung it open and was gone.

Several little children tottered after her and started crying when Tracy closed the door. The demanding toddler grabbed Ellen's leg and started up his chant of, "Fwo! Fwo! Fwo!" He seemed to expect her to start where Mirror-Belle had left off.

"I'm sorry about all that," said Ellen to Tracy.

"Don't worry," said Tracy. "We can't choose our families."

Ellen decided it would be useless to explain again that Mirror-Belle wasn't related to her. Instead she helped Tracy pick up the scattered balls and throw them back into the ball pool. The toddlers didn't seem to enjoy this nearly as much as they had enjoyed Mirror-Belle throwing them all out, and the crying grew louder.

"Well, I'd better go," said Ellen when the last ball was back in the pool. She wondered where Mirror-Belle had got to but decided not to look for her this time. She would go and find Dad and Luke on their squash court.

She didn't need to. As soon as she opened the door she saw them outside in the corridor.

"So that's where you've been hiding," said Dad.

Luke was looking cross. "Give it back," he said.

"What are you talking about?" asked Ellen.

"The squash ball, of course. That yellow one was our best one. It was really bouncy."

"But I haven't got it."

"Then what have you done with it?"

"Nothing. I never had it."

"Yes, you did – you came rushing in and snatched it."

"It wasn't me. It must have been Mirror-Belle. She was looking for the magic ball, you see – the one her fairy godmother threw – and—"

"Oh shut up." Luke turned to Dad. "She's always telling whoppers."

But Dad was in a surprisingly good mood. "Ellen's got a vivid imagination, that's all," he said. "And it's not as if that yellow ball was ours anyway. We just found it on the court when we arrived."

Luke didn't want to give up so easily. "She's hidden it in the kids' gym some-where," he said. "I'm sure I saw her go in there."

Ellen guessed that Mirror-Belle had run back to the gym with the squash ball – or was it really the magic ball? In either case, she had probably taken it back to her own land through one of the mirrors in the gym. But Ellen knew that to say so would be the wrong thing. It would only make Luke even crosser. So instead she asked, "Who won at squash?"

Luke scowled. That seemed to be the wrong thing too.

"I did," said Dad.

Chapter Three

The Sea Monster's Cave

"For goodness sake," said Ellen impatiently to her big brother, who was pushing yet another coin into his favourite seaside slot machine. "I bet Granny and Grandpa wouldn't want you to waste all their money on that thing."

"I'm not wasting it. I'm going to end up with more than I started with." Luke's teeth were gritted and his eyes had a determined gleam. "Can't you see, that whole pile of coins is about to tumble off the edge. Then I'll win them all! I'll probably win them next go." But he didn't; or the next go or the one after that.

They had been on holiday for a week, staying in a caravan park with their grandparents. Granny and Grandpa had gone out for a last row in their boat and had given Luke and Ellen ten pounds spending money each.

"I'm sick of hanging around waiting for you," Ellen complained. "At this rate I won't get to the shops at all. Don't forget, they're taking us out this afternoon, and tomorrow we're going home."

"Well, why don't I see you back here in an hour," suggested Luke, and Ellen agreed, even though she knew he had promised to look after her.

There were two gift shops by the beach. Ellen wandered round one of them and chose a packet of sparkly pens and a little notepad with a picture of a seal and "Best wishes from Whitesands" on the front. She paid for them and put them in her backpack, along with her sun lotion.

She still had six pounds left so she went into the second shop, which sold all sorts of ornamental sea creatures – fish, lobsters and sea horses – as well as boxes covered in shiny shells. Most things were too expensive, but Ellen enjoyed looking round. Tucked away in a corner she found a beautiful mirror decorated round the outside with a mermaid and shells. It cost £9.99, and Ellen began to wish she hadn't bought the things in the first shop. She was just wondering whether she could take them back when a voice from the mermaid mirror said,

"So it *is* you! I nearly didn't recognize you under all those freckles."

"Mirror-Belle!" Ellen hadn't seen her mirror friend all holidays and felt quite pleased to see her now, even though she knew there was bound to be trouble in store. "You've got lots of freckles too," she said.

"Don't be silly – they're not freckles, they're beauty spots," replied Princess Mirror-Belle, and she dived out of the mirror, landing on her hands with her legs in the air.

The shop assistant must have heard the thud. She left the customer she was serving and hurried over to them, looking cross.

"Please don't do handstands in here," she said

to Mirror-Belle. "You might break something."

"It wasn't a handstand. It was a dive," said Mirror-Belle, on her feet by now. "With all these sea creatures around, I naturally assumed I would land in the sea. It's extremely confusing; I suggest you remove them and put some land animals on the shelves instead."

"Why don't you go and play on the beach?" said the shop assistant.

"I didn't hear you say, 'Your Royal Highness'," objected Mirror-Belle, "but it's quite a good idea, so I'll excuse you just this once. Come on, Ellen."

"Sorry," Ellen murmured to the assistant, and she followed Mirror-Belle out of the shop and on to the beach.

Three children were digging in the sand. Mirror-Belle went up to them.

"I doubt if you'll find any treasure here," she said. "The sea monster is

much more likely to have hidden it in a cave, and he's probably guarding it."

The children just stared at her.

"They're not digging for treasure – they're building a sandcastle," Ellen told Mirror-Belle.

"What a ridiculous idea! You can't build a castle out of sand. I should know, I live in one."

"I thought you lived in a palace," said Ellen.

"That's in the winter. In the summer we go to our castle by the sea. It's made of pure white marble with ivory towers." Mirror-Belle turned back to the children. "In any case, you shouldn't build it on the beach. Don't you realize it will collapse when the tide comes in?"

"We don't mind," said one of them. "We'll have gone home by then."

"What? You're building a castle and you're not even going to live in it?" Mirror-Belle shook her head pityingly. "There's no hope for them, Ellen. We'd better move on," she said.

"Shall we look for shells?" suggested Ellen as they walked along between the sea and the row of beach umbrellas.

Instead of answering her, Mirror-Belle gazed at the sky and then marched up to the nearest umbrella. A man and a woman were dozing underneath it.

"Allow me," said Mirror-Belle, and she

stepped over them and closed the umbrella.

"Hey, what are you doing?" said the woman, sitting up.

"What does it look like?" answered Mirror-Belle. "There's not a trace of rain, so you really don't need an umbrella."

The man was on his feet by this time. "Buzz off," he said as he opened the umbrella up again.

"I'm a princess, not a bee," replied Mirror-Belle.

Ellen tugged at her arm and Mirror-Belle allowed herself to be pulled away, but not without saying in a loud voice, "I'm beginning to wonder if this is a special beach for idiots."

"They're not idiots," Ellen told her off when they were out of earshot. "They just don't want to get sunburned. That reminds me, I ought to put some lotion on." She took the bottle out of her back-pack. "It's to protect me against the sun," she explained, and then realized that Mirror-Belle had an identical bag on her back. "Haven't you got some too?"

"Not exactly" said Mirror-Belle, open-ing her own bag. Ellen looked inside and saw some sparkly pens and a notepad just like the ones she had just bought. Mirror-Belle took out a bottle and unscrewed the cap. "This is to protect me against sea monsters," she said as she smeared some of it over her neck and arms.

Ellen laughed. "I don't think you get sea monsters in Whitesands," she said.

"I wouldn't be so sure," replied Mirror-Belle dark-ly. She screwed up her eyes and looked out to sea. "I can't see any," she admitted, "though I can see some rather ugly mermaids on that rock. Their tails look all right, but why haven't they got long golden hair?"

Ellen looked too and laughed again. "Those aren't mermaids – they're seals," she said.

"Well, give me mermaids any day," replied Mirror-Belle. "The rocks near our castle are covered in them."

"Do you play with them?" asked Ellen, though she wasn't really sure if she believed in these mermaids.

"Sometimes. It's not much fun though, because they spend so much time combing their hair." Mirror-Belle paused for a moment and then added, "One of them gave me a magic comb for my birthday."

"What was magic about it?" asked Ellen.

"It could change your hair into any style you wished for. The colour too. I once had purple ringlets down to my toes."

"Have you still got the comb?"

"Really, Ellen, I wish you wouldn't always ask so many questions. If you must know, it was stolen by a sea monster."

"Are sea monsters hairy then?"

"Of course. I thought even you would know that."

They reached the rocky end of the beach, where there were fewer people. They picked seaweed off the rocks and made necklaces with it and a crown for Mirror-Belle, who said, "It's a shame you can't have one too, Ellen, but the only way you could become a princess would be to marry a prince."

They wandered along the curved shore further than Ellen had ever been before.

There were cliffs behind them now and they had to clamber over boulders. They reached the tip of the bay and carried on into the next one.

"Look!" said Mirror-Belle, pointing to an opening at the foot of a cliff. "That's the entrance to a cave. I wonder if it belongs to the sea monster. Would you like some of my protective lotion, Ellen?"

"All right," said Ellen, just to keep Mirror-Belle happy. She was pretty sure that sea monsters didn't exist; at least, they might do in Mirror-Belle's world, but not here in Whitesands.

The cave, when they reached it, was disappointing. It was quite small and empty, except for a couple of cans and a lemonade bottle. "No sign of any sea monster," said Ellen.

"On the contrary." Mirror-Belle had picked up the empty lemonade bottle and was looking excited. "Didn't you know, they love lemonade? If they don't drink lots of it, they lose their slime."

"I thought you said they were hairy," Ellen objected, but Mirror-Belle didn't seem to have heard her. She was examining some writing on the wall of the cave. Ellen looked too and saw that a lot of people had carved their names into the rock. "Look at this!" said Mirror-Belle, pointing to some rather wiggly letters which said: "T. Box 1.8.01."

"What about it?" asked Ellen.

"Can't you see? It's a clue. The 'T' must stand for treasure."

"It probably stands for Tom or Tessa or something," said Ellen. "And Box is their surname."

"The poor creature has written it back to front," Mirror-Belle carried on, ignoring Ellen, "but then sea monsters aren't very intelligent. Never mind – look at those numbers, Ellen: they're the important thing. They show us where the treasure box is buried."

"I think they're just the date," said Ellen. "'1.8.01' means the first of August, 2001. That's when this Box person carved their name."

"Nothing of the sort," scoffed Mirror-Belle. "It means that we have to take one step in one direction, eight steps in

another direction and then dig one foot underground."

Ellen frowned doubtfully. This wasn't the first time Mirror-Belle had been so excited about treasure. Ellen remembered when she had claimed that her dog, Prince Precious Paws, could sniff out gold and jewels, but he hadn't succeeded.

"Don't look so gloomy, Ellen," Mirror-Belle reproached her. "You should be even happier than I am! After all, I'm incredibly rich already, but think what a difference all this wealth will make to you."

This reminded Ellen of Luke and all the coins in the slot machine.

"Help!" she said. "I must go. Luke will be getting worried – and I expect Granny and Grandpa will be back by now. Are you coming?"

"Of course not. Can't you see, this is the perfect opportunity to dig up the treasure, when the sea monster isn't guarding it."

"Do be careful, Mirror-Belle," said Ellen and then had to remind herself that sea monsters didn't really exist.

"Oh, I'll be fine. I've got my protective lotion, remember. But I'm surprised that you're leaving me to do all the digging by myself. Just think – there might even be a magic comb buried with all the gold and jewels. You'd like that, wouldn't you?"

But Ellen couldn't be persuaded. She hurried back over the rocks and along the beach. She found Luke pacing about outside the arcade of slot machines.

"Thank goodness you're back," he said. "They'd go mad if I'd lost you."

"Sorry," said Ellen. "I've been with Mirror-Belle."

"Oh, do shut up blaming everything on someone who doesn't even exist,"

Luke snapped at her. Ellen decided that now wasn't the best moment to ask him if he'd won any money, but from the expression on his face she doubted it.

That afternoon Granny and Grandpa took them out to a bird sanctuary, and they all had supper in a cafe on the way home.

"You're very quiet, Ellen, pet," said Granny.

"She's tired," said Grandpa, but it wasn't that. Ellen couldn't help thinking about Mirror-Belle and hoping she was all right. Was she still in the cave or had she returned to her own world? Ellen half expected to find her waiting for them when they got back to the camper van, but she wasn't.

"Early to bed and early to rise," said Granny after the game of cards they always played in the evening. "We've got a long journey tomorrow."

But Ellen couldn't sleep. She lay awake in the camper van listening to her grandparents' gentle snores and worrying about Mirror-Belle. If only there was someone she could talk to! She wondered if Luke was still awake. He didn't sleep in the camper van but in a tent just outside.

Ellen put her anorak on over her pyjamas and slipped on her flip-flops. Quietly she opened the door of the camper van and stepped outside. It was a clear night and the moon was nearly full.

"Luke!" she whispered. She unzipped his tent a few inches and whispered again. There was no reply. Ellen knew he would only be cross if she woke him. She really should go back to bed, but instead she found herself walking down to the little beach where Granny and Grandpa moored their rowing boat.

She looked out to sea. She could see

the cliffs at the end of the bay, where she and Mirror-Belle had walked that morning, but now the tide was high, covering the boulders where they had clambered.

The next bay, the one with the cave in it, must be cut off by the tide. If Mirror-Belle was still in the cave, she would be trapped. And there wasn't a mirror there for her to escape into.

A breeze blew in from the sea and Ellen shivered. She thought of Mirror-Belle with no anorak to keep her warm. She wouldn't have had anything to eat either. And if she really did believe in sea monsters, she might be feeling scared as well as cold and hungry.

Then Ellen noticed something bobbing in the water. It was a plastic lemonade bottle. It looked as if there was something inside it: a scrap of paper.

Ellen rolled up her pyjama trousers, took a couple of steps into the cold water and reached out for the bottle. She unscrewed the top. Sure enough, there was a rolled-up piece of paper inside it. When Ellen unrolled it and saw the glittery backwards writing she knew at once who the message was from. This is what it said:

HELP! I AM TRAPPED IN THE SEA MONSTER'S CAVE. I NEED A NICE PRINCE TO RESCUE ME. THE REWARD WILL BE HALF MY FATHER'S KINGDOM AND MY HAND IN MARRIAGE (WHEN I AM OLD ENOUGH).

PRINCESS MIRROR-BELLE
XXX

Ellen was very good at reading backwards writing after all her adventures with Mirror-Belle, so she read it as:

HELP! I AM TRAPPED IN THE SEA
MONSTER'S CAVE. I NEED A NICE
PRINCE TO RESCUE ME. THE REWARD
WILL BE HALF MY FATHER'S KINGDOM
AND MY HAND IN MARRIAGE (WHEN I
AM OLD ENOUGH).

PRINCESS MIRROR-BELLE
XXX

"There it is!" Ellen pointed at the dark
gap in the cliff face.

"This had better not be a trick," said
Luke, who was rowing the boat.

It had been easier than Ellen had
imagined to wake him
and talk him into this
night-time boat trip.
Luke had always
liked adventures,
and although he
had never before
believed in

Mirror-Belle, the back-to-front note in the bottle had seemed to convince him.

The sea was calm and the moon was bright, so it hadn't taken them long to row round into the next bay. Ellen was relieved to see that there was a strip of sand in front of the cave; at least it wasn't flooded.

"Look!" She stood up and pointed again in great excitement.

"Sit down – you're rocking the boat," said Luke. He was rowing with his back to the cliffs and couldn't see what Ellen could see – a pale figure standing in the mouth of the cave.

"Mirror-Belle!" she called out.

A few minutes later Mirror-Belle was climbing into the boat.

"Hello, Ellen," she said, and then, "My prince! My hero!" she greeted Luke.

"He's not a prince. He's just my brother," said Ellen.

"Never mind. He will be a prince once he marries me, won't you, my brave rescuer?" She flung her arms round Luke, who wriggled awkwardly out of her grasp. One of her seaweed necklaces had come off and stuck to him and he threw it into the sea.

"Settle down, you girls," he said, and picked up the oars.

"It's a pity you didn't get the chance to slay the sea monster," said Mirror-Belle. "I can't think where he can have got to."

Ellen was surprised that Mirror-Belle was in such a perky mood after being trapped in the cave for so long. "Did you find any treasure?" she asked.

But Mirror-Belle only seemed to want to talk to Luke. "Which half of my father's kingdom would you like?" she asked him as the boat bobbed along. "One half is covered in mountains and the other half is full of deep lakes."

Luke didn't reply but Mirror-Belle was not put out. She picked up the lemonade bottle with the note in it from the floor of the boat. "My father might ask a few questions about you at first, but I'm sure I can make him see reason if I show him this," she said.

Ellen was beginning to feel annoyed. "It was me who found that, you know, not Luke. I've been worrying and worrying about you."

But Mirror-Belle's mind was still full of the marriage arrangements. "I suppose we'll have to wait about ten years," she said to Luke. "You could be learning a few princely things in the meantime, like hunting dragons and cutting off trolls' heads. Would you rather do that here or would you like to come back with me and have some lessons in the palace?"

"I'm trying to concentrate on the rowing," said Luke. Ellen could tell from his voice that he felt embarrassed.

"Luke doesn't want to get married," she told Mirror-Belle. "All he cares about is his band."

"That's not a problem," said Mirror-Belle. "He could be in a band of princes. They could be called the Dragon Slayers or the Royal Rescuers . . . or the Handsome Heroes." She turned back to Luke. "How would you like to play a golden guitar?"

"Am I just dreaming this?" Luke muttered.

They had reached the caravan park beach.

"I'll tie up the boat," said Luke as they clambered out. Mirror-Belle tried again to hug him, but he shrugged her off.

"Do you want to sleep in the camper van with me?" asked Ellen. "You'll have to be quiet, so as not to disturb Granny and Grandpa."

But Mirror-Belle didn't like this idea. "I'll sleep under the stars," she said. "Then I can guard my hero's tent in case the sea monster comes to take revenge."

"You'd better have my anorak then," said Ellen.

Luke offered rather reluctantly to sleep outside himself and let Mirror-Belle have the tent but she refused. "You've been enough of a hero for one night," she told him. "It's my turn to be a heroine."

"Your tea's cold," said Granny to Ellen the next morning. "I've tried to wake you about five times."

Ellen sat up in bed and noticed that Granny was holding her anorak.

"I found this on the ground outside," she said.

"Was Mirror-Belle there?" asked Ellen. "She said she wanted to sleep under the stars."

Granny chuckled. "That's some dream you've been having."

Grandpa came in. "That's it – I've fixed the boat to the tow bar," he said. "I was hoping that brother of yours would help me, but he's dead to the world."

"Shall we leave him behind, Ellen? What do you think?" joked Granny. But Ellen was thinking more about Mirror-Belle than about Luke. As soon as she was dressed she went outside to look for her. Luke was just staggering, bleary-eyed, out of his tent.

"Mirror-Belle seems to have gone," said Ellen.

Luke looked blank for a second and

then scratched his head. "That's funny – I had a dream about Mirror-Belle," he said. "Something about a message in a bottle and rescuing her in a boat."

"It wasn't a dream. It was real!" Ellen protested. "I can show you the bottle and the message!" But then she remembered that Mirror-Belle had taken them.

Grandpa appeared at the doorway of the camper van. "Good afternoon," he said to Luke, though it was only half past nine. "You'd better start taking that tent down. Everything else is packed up."

He gave the windows of the camper van a loving wipe and then made a tut-tutting noise.

"What's the matter?" asked Luke.

"Someone's been fiddling about with the wing mirror. It's all bent back."

Grandpa straightened it out and then said, "That's funny."

"What is?" Ellen asked.

"There's seaweed all over it," said Grandpa.

Chapter Four

The Unusual Pets Club

"Do you want to come back to my house for tea?" Ellen asked her best friend, Katy. They were in the school playground.

"I can't. I'm going to the Unusual Pets Club."

"What's that?"

"I don't really know much about it. It's the first meeting tonight, at Crystal's house. Hasn't she asked you too?"

"No." Ellen felt cross. Crystal was a bossy girl in their class who was always starting up clubs and societies and then meanly not letting everyone join.

"You have to have an unusual pet to join it," said Katy. "Maybe you could bring Splodge along. Shall I ask Crystal?"

Ellen didn't know what to say. She wanted to pretend that she didn't care about the stupid old club, but in fact it sounded quite fun.

Just then, Crystal came up to them.

"Hi, Katy," she said. "Do you know how to get to my house?"

"I think so," said Katy. "Can Ellen come too?"

Crystal looked doubtful. "Well, I don't know. I didn't think you had an unusual pet, Ellen."

"She's got Splodge," said Katy. "He's a really nice dog. He's brilliant at chasing sticks and bringing them back, isn't he, Ellen?"

"But all dogs can do that," objected Crystal. "There's nothing unusual about it."

"What sort of unusual things do you mean?" asked Ellen. As far as she knew, Crystal's hamster, Silver, was perfectly normal.

But Crystal obviously didn't think so. "Well, like Silver, for instance," she said. "You know hamsters have two pouches in their cheeks and they stuff food in them? Well, Silver only ever uses his right pouch, never the left one – it's amazing!"

"And Twiglet can do this sort of dance," said Katy. Twiglet was her stick insect, and it was true that sometimes he moved from side to side in quite a rhythmic way, whereas most stick insects stayed still all the time.

"I tell you what, Ellen," said Crystal graciously. "See if you can teach Splodge a trick or something after school, and then you can bring him along at six o'clock. But it will be a sort of trial. If he's not unusual enough then he can't come to any of the other meetings."

When Ellen got home she found her old hula hoop and took Splodge out into the garden. She held the hoop out in front of him and said, "Jump!"

But Splodge didn't understand; he just sat looking up at her eagerly as if he expected her to throw the hoop for him. Ellen had to give up on that trick.

She didn't succeed any better when she tried to teach Splodge to stand up and beg, or to thump his tail three times when she asked how old he was. The only thing he would do was shake hands, but Ellen didn't think Crystal would call that unusual enough.

A spider scuttled over Ellen's shoe and suddenly she had an idea. Her brother Luke had a pet tarantula called Evilton. A tarantula would surely count as an unusual pet.

She ran into the house with Splodge at her heels. Luke was sprawled on the sofa watching the music channel on television.

"Can I borrow Evilton?" asked Ellen breathlessly.

"Be quiet – this is Fire Engine's new release." Luke turned the volume up and sang along with the band:

"So you think you can ride the storm,
    babe,
And there's nothing you can't do
But I can see a big wave coming
And it's gonna crash over you."

Ellen fidgeted impatiently till at last the song came to an end. Then she asked him again.

"Please, Luke. Just for this evening. I want to take him to the Unusual Pets Club."

"No," said Luke. "I'm not having Evilton join some silly girly club."

"It's not just for girls. Martin Booth is bringing his slow-worm. Oh, go on, Luke!"

"No," said Luke. "Evilton might catch cold. Anyway, I need him to help me with my homework!" He laughed as if this was hilarious, and when Ellen tried to argue he turned the volume up even louder. Fire Engine was singing another song.

Suddenly Ellen realized that she had missed most of her favourite programme, *Holiday Swap*. She picked up the remote control, but Luke snatched it back.

"You're so mean," said Ellen. "This

stuff is on twenty-four hours a day, and *Holiday Swap* only lasts half an hour."

"I got here first," said Luke, and he made her wait while the band was interviewed before he handed over the control. "OK – it's all yours," he said at last, and went out of the room, leaving the door open.

Ellen switched channels. *Holiday Swap* had just finished.

"I hate you," she shouted after Luke. She turned the television off angrily. Splodge laid his chin on her lap and she stroked his head. "You're the only nice one," she told him.

"What about me?" came a ghostly whisper. The voice sounded slightly familiar, and for a moment Ellen wondered if it was Mirror-Belle. But there was no mirror in the room, and anyway the voice was too soft to be Mirror-Belle's.

Splodge had heard the mysterious whisper too, and he didn't like it. He whined and hid behind the sofa, leaving Ellen to stare at the television, which is where the voice seemed to have come from. And yet she had definitely turned it off – the screen was dull and blank. Actually, that wasn't quite true: Ellen could just see herself in it, but it wasn't what she would call a proper reflection; it was faint and grey and transparent.

"Happy Throughsday," whispered the faint grey transparent person, and stepped out of the television.

"Mirror-Belle – it is you! But you look all funny – like a ghost! I can see right through you."

"Well, what do you expect on Throughsday?" said Princess Mirror-Belle. Her voice was a little louder now, more of an eerie chant than a whisper.

"You sound funny too. And what do you mean – Throughsday? It's Thursday today."

"It may be Thursday here, but back home it's Throughsday," said Mirror-Belle. "Everyone can walk through things on Throughsday. Like this." And she walked through the sofa. Splodge growled.

"That's amazing!" said Ellen. "Can you go through doors too?"

"Naturally, but someone seems to have left this one open."

"That's Luke. He's so irritating." Ellen closed the door and watched as

Mirror-Belle glided through it and back again.

Splodge barked furiously.

"It's a pity you can't keep him under better control," said Mirror-Belle. "Still, I suppose I shouldn't expect your dog to be as well behaved as mine, seeing that he doesn't have any royal blood."

In fact, Mirror-Belle's dog, Prince Precious Paws, was the worst-behaved pet Ellen had ever met. She remembered the time he had stolen a roast chicken and scared a lot of sheep, but she decided not to mention this. Instead, now that they were on the subject of dogs, she found herself telling Mirror-Belle all about the Unusual Pets Club and how annoying Crystal was.

"And Luke's been horrible too," she said. "Everyone seems to be against me."

A thoughtful look crossed Mirror-Belle's face. "I can change that," she

said, and she walked through the television.

Splodge began to bark at the television
as if this should have stopped Mirror-
Belle.

"Calm down," Ellen told him, but
Mirror-Belle said, "He needs to look at
the television. It's part of the plan."

Just then, a strange echoey barking sound came from the screen.

"Here he comes, the
dear sweet creature,"
Mirror-Belle said,
and the next second
a ghostly Prince
Precious Paws
bounded out of the
screen and into the room.

"There's your unusual pet," said
Mirror-Belle to Ellen. "At least, he's
mine, really, but I'll let you borrow him."

Luke was hungry. Supper wouldn't be for ages: Mum was still teaching the piano. He opened the kitchen cupboard and found a jar of salsa.

"But I can see a big wave coming

And it's gonna crash over you," he sang as he rummaged around some more. That Fire Engine song was so brilliant. Luke wished he could write something as good as that for his own band, Breakneck.

He discovered a bag of rather stale crisps and dipped one into the bright red salsa. Suddenly he felt inspired. "Red, the colour of anger," he said to himself. That would be a good first line. How could the song go after that?

"Red, the colour of anger,

Blue, the colour of sorrow . . ." he sang with his mouth full. He was pausing to think what could come next, when a soft, eerie voice behind him sang:

"And green for the mean, mean brother
Who wouldn't let his sister borrow."

Luke looked over his shoulder and saw Ellen. At least, he thought he saw her, but the next second she had gone. She seemed to have disappeared through the wall. But of course she couldn't have done that.

"Ellen!" Luke strode out of the kitchen and into the television room. Only Splodge was there, sitting in front of the television and staring at the blank screen. Ellen was probably hiding somewhere, giggling. Oh well, he wouldn't give her the satisfaction of looking for her. Better make a start on his homework.

Up in his room, Luke found it hard to concentrate on the Second World War. He kept thinking about Ellen and feeling a bit guilty that he hadn't let her borrow his pet.

Evilton was burrowing about in the

bark chippings inside his tank on Luke's table. As Luke watched him the words of a new song began to form themselves in his mind.

"You just want to poison me
But I'm not gonna let you start . . . "

He chewed his pen and wondered how to carry on. Then his skin prickled as he heard the same ghostly voice as before.

"You just want to poison me
And I'm dying of a broken heart."

Luke jumped up and turned round. There stood Ellen, and yet he hadn't heard her come into the room.

"Ellen – why can't you knock before you . . . " Luke's voice trailed off and he stared at his sister. With a cold shock, he realized he could see right through her.

"Ellen, what's the matter . . . you look all . . . You look like a . . . " Luke couldn't bring himself to say the word "ghost".

The ghostly girl gave a small sad

smile. "I forgive you," she said, "but can you forgive yourself?"

Luke gaped. The girl was stepping backwards, still fixing him with her haunting gaze. Then, before he could think what to say, she had vanished through his bedroom wall.

He shivered. What was happening?

"Ellen! Come back!" But had it been Ellen?

Maybe Luke had just been thinking so deeply about his new song that he had somehow imagined his sister's ghost. But why? It was strange, even frightening.

Luke searched the house. He could hear piano music coming from the sitting room, and in the television room Splodge was still staring at the blank screen, but there was no sign of Ellen. The more Luke thought about her the more he wished he had been nicer to her.

Then he saw the note on the hall table. "Gone to the Unusual Pets Club," it said.

So that was all right then. Or was it?

"Right, everyone's here," said Crystal.

"Except for Ellen," said Katy.

"Well, we'll just have to start without her."

Crystal's front room looked like a vet's waiting room. Five children were sitting around with their pets either on their knees or in boxes or cages beside them. Crystal, in the biggest armchair, had to keep moving one hand in front of the other as her hamster Silver ran over them.

"Welcome to the Unusual Pets Club," she said. "We'll take turns to introduce our pets, and then at the end of the meeting we'll vote for the most unusual one. The winner will get this special certificate." She let Katy take Silver while she held out a piece of paper with "Most Unusual Pet of the Week" written on it in big purple letters.

"But won't the same pet just win every week?" asked Martin Booth, whose pet slow-worm was draped contentedly round his neck.

"Not necessarily. New people might join, or someone might get a new pet, or ... well, some pets might just become more unusual. Now, we'll go round in a circle, starting with me." Crystal took Silver back from Katy and explained about his unusual feeding habits. She gave him two pieces of carrot, and sure enough he stuffed them both into his right pouch. Some people clapped, and Crystal smiled smugly.

"You next, Rachel."

Rachel had brought a Siamese cat who was sitting on her knee.

"This is Lapsang," she said. "She's got a very unusual miaow."

"What's unusual about it?" demanded Crystal.

"It's very low. She sounds more like a dog than a cat."

"But all Siamese cats have low voices," said Martin.

"Not as low as Lapsang's," said Rachel.

"Let's hear it then," Crystal ordered.

"Go on, Lapsang – miaow!" Rachel jiggled her legs, disturbing Lapsang's comfortable position. The cat looked offended, jumped off Rachel's lap and stalked silently to the door.

"She'll probably do it later," said

Rachel, looking plead-
ingly at Crystal.

"She'll have to,
otherwise you can't
stay in the club," said
Crystal. She turned to
Martin. "Your turn."

"This is Sinclair,"
said Martin, unwinding
his slow-worm from his neck
and holding him out. Some of the other
children backed away.

"Is he poisonous?" asked Rachel.

Martin gave her a scornful look. "No.
He's not a snake. He's a slow-worm.
That's a type of lizard – a legless lizard,"
he said triumphantly.

Everyone looked impressed apart from
Crystal, who said, "Well, go on then. Tell
us what's unusual about him."

"I've just told you. He hasn't got any
legs. Most lizards have legs, don't they?"

"Yes, but slow-worms don't," pointed out Katy. "I think Sinclair would be more unusual if he did have legs."

An argument broke out, with the children taking sides. Crystal had to call the meeting to order.

"We can have the discussion and the vote at the end," she said. "Now, tell us about your guinea pig, Pamina."

"She's got very unusual fur," said Pamina, producing a mangy-looking ginger guinea-pig from a box of straw. "And she's also got a very unusual name – Timbucktoodle-oo."

"Names don't count," Crystal told her. "Tell us what's unusual about the fur."

"Well, you can see," said Pamina. "It's got all these bald patches."

"I don't call that properly unusual," said Crystal. "I'd say she's just got some kind of disease. You ought to take her to the vet. Now, Katy, it's your turn."

But before Katy's stick insect had a chance to show off its dancing talent, there was a ring at the door.

Crystal went to answer it. "Hello, Ellen. You're a bit late," the others heard her say, and the next second a strange-looking dog bounded into the room.

Lapsang's fur stood on end and she at last demonstrated her low-pitched miaow, but this didn't put the new unusual pet off: he made a dash for the cat, who fled across the room and up the curtains.

"Come here, Prince Precious . . . I mean, Splodge!" commanded Ellen, but the dog ignored her. He had spotted Silver the hamster and was leaping up at Crystal. Everyone gasped: for one second it looked as if his jaws had actually closed round the hamster. But a moment later the dog had bounded back to Ellen and Silver was still running about over Crystal's hands.

"Being unusually badly-behaved doesn't count," said Crystal.

"Is Splodge all right?" Katy asked Ellen. "He looks all different – sort of see-through."

"That's his new trick," said Ellen. "He can turn himself into a ghost dog."

Just then the dog gave a growl which was more like the rustle of autumn leaves. He was staring at Sinclair the slow-worm and his ghostly hair was bristling. He backed away, then turned and ran.

"He's gone through the wall!" exclaimed Rachel.

"He couldn't have done," said Crystal.

"He has," said Ellen. "He

can do that. He's a very, very unusual pet."

"There he is – he's looking in through the window!" said Martin.

Lapsang gave another deep miaow, then jumped down from the curtain and slunk into her cat basket.

"Call him back inside, Ellen," said Katy.

"I don't think he'll come if Sinclair is still out," said Ellen.

Martin obligingly put Sinclair into his tank and covered it with his jacket. Meanwhile Rachel put Timbucktoodle-oo back into his box and Crystal shut Silver into his cage. Then Ellen called, "Splodge! Splodge!" and the ghost dog came bounding in through the closed window.

Everyone laughed and clapped. After that the children had fun getting Ellen's unusual pet to go through various bits of furniture.

"He can even go through people!" boasted Ellen. They all stood in a line, shoulder to shoulder, and sure enough the wildly excited dog jumped through the human wall and back again. After a few goes of this, he leaped through the window again.

"What's he up to now?" said Pamina.

They all crowded to the window. Crystal's little brother was outside, playing football with some friends. The ghost dog was trying to get the ball, but of course his jaws just kept going through it.

"Come back!" Ellen called. The dog turned and gave her a cheeky look, and then he bounded off down the road. She guessed he was going back to his true owner but she didn't tell the others.

"As he's not here any more, no one's allowed to vote for him," said Crystal, but for once the others rose up against her: "That's not fair." "He was at the meeting." "He's so unusual!"

Crystal had to give in. "All right. But remember," and she glared at Ellen, "no one is allowed to vote for their own pet."

The vote took place, and there was no doubt about the winner. Twiglet the stick insect got two votes (from Crystal and Ellen); everyone else voted for the ghost dog.

Rather grumpily, Crystal handed Ellen the certificate. "I hope you realize that the winner has to have the next meeting in their house. It's in the rules," she said.

"That should be fine," said Ellen, "but I don't know if Splodge will be able to do his ghost trick next week. He only does it some- times."

Everyone except Crystal looked disap-pointed.

Back home, Ellen had a quick look round for the mirror girl and dog, but there was no sign of them and Mum was calling her to supper.

"Pass the potatoes, please, Ellen," said Luke. "Did you have a good time at the club?" He sounded surprisingly polite.

"Yes, thanks," said Ellen frostily. She still hadn't forgiven him for his behaviour earlier.

"What club?" asked Dad, so Ellen told them a bit about the meeting. She didn't mention Prince Precious Paws. Her fam-ily didn't even believe in Mirror-Belle, so she reckoned that a ghost dog would be too much for them to swallow. Instead she pretended that she had just gone along to watch.

"Why didn't you take Splodge with you?" asked Mum.

"He's not unusual enough," Ellen explained. "But maybe I'll be able to teach him a couple of tricks by next week. The meeting's supposed to be here at six o'clock – is that all right?"

Mum agreed, and Luke said, "That's good. You'll have time to watch *Holiday Swap* first."

Ellen gave him a suspicious look. "Why are you being so nice all of a sudden?" she asked. "What's got into you?"

"Just toad-in-the-hole," said Luke, holding out his plate for a second helping.

"Talking of television," said Dad, "Splodge was behaving very oddly when I was watching the news just now. He kept barking at the television, as if it was going to bite him. And then I noticed that the screen had paw prints on it, as if he'd been attacking it – all very weird."

Ellen smiled. She knew who the paw prints really belonged to. Prince Precious Paws must have gone back through the screen with Mirror-Belle. She felt sorry not to have said goodbye.

"Well, Ellen?" said Luke, breaking into her secret thoughts, and Ellen realized he had been talking to her.

"Sorry, I wasn't concentrating."

"I was just saying," said Luke, "that I've been thinking about Evilton. If you want to borrow him next week, that's fine by me."

Chapter Five

The Sleepwalking Beauty

Christmas pudding or Sleeping Beauty?
That was the question Ellen was asking
herself as she wrapped up a present for
her best friend Katy.

It was Christmas Eve, and Katy was
having a fancy dress party. Ellen couldn't
decide what to go as. She had already
worn the Christmas pudding costume in
the end-of-term ballet show. It had a wire
frame which was quite uncomfortable
and meant you couldn't sit down. Still, it
did look good, especially the little cap
with the sprig of holly on it.

The Sleeping Beauty costume wasn't

so Christmassy. It was just a lacy white Victorian nightdress Ellen's mother had bought at a car-boot sale. But it was very pretty, and Ellen decided to wear it if she could find something else to go with it.

As soon as she had finished wrapping up the present she tried on the night-dress. Looking through her dressing-up box she found an old net curtain which she draped over her head. She fixed it into place with a gold-coloured plastic headband which looked quite like a crown. There was a pair of very long white button-up gloves in the box too. Mum had told her that her great-grandmother used to wear them for going to balls. Ellen put them on and then went to see how the whole outfit looked in her wardrobe mirror.

She should have known better, of course.

"I don't see why you need to bother with gloves," said Princess Mirror-Belle, looking at her critically from the mirror. "After all, what would it matter if you pricked your finger?"

Ellen was dismayed. "Oh, Mirror-Belle, this isn't a good time to come!" she said.

"What do you mean?" said Mirror-Belle, looking offended. "Surely you'd rather play with a princess than by yourself?"

"But I'm not going to be by myself. I'm just off to Katy's party. This is my Sleeping Beauty costume."

Mirror-Belle laughed. "Poor you, having to dress up as a Sleeping Beauty, when I really am one," she said.

"No you're not – you're Mirror-Belle."

"Of course – and 'Belle' means 'Beauty'. I thought everyone knew that. Have you forgotten what I told you the very first time we met?"

Ellen thought back. She did seem to remember some story about Mirror-Belle's wicked fairy godmother pricking her finger and sending her to sleep for a very long time. But then Mirror-Belle was always telling her stories and Ellen never knew how many of them were true.

Mirror-Belle had stepped out of the mirror and was looking round Ellen's bedroom. Her eyes fell on the cap belonging to the Christmas pudding costume.

"It's very careless of you to leave that holly lying around," she said. "Suppose I pricked my finger on it?"

"It's not real holly," said Ellen. "It's just made of plastic. And I don't know what you're so worried about. I thought you'd already gone to sleep for a hundred years."

"Two hundred," Mirror-Belle corrected her. "So what?"

"Well, you woke up in the end, didn't you? So the spell must be broken."

"You obviously don't know my wicked fairy godmother," said Mirror-Belle. "I'm in danger every day of my life. The next time I prick my finger it's going to happen all over again, only this time it could be for three hundred years. That's why I always wear gloves."

Ellen was sure she hadn't ever seen Mirror-Belle wearing gloves before, but she didn't want to start arguing about that now. "Well, anyway, Mirror-Belle, the party will be starting soon. I'll have to go."

"Don't you mean 'We'?" asked Mirror-Belle, looking offended again.

"No, I don't. I'm sorry, but it would all be too complicated. Everyone would keep thinking you were me, or my twin or something, and I'm just not in the mood for that."

"Aha!" Mirror-Belle flipped her net curtain over her head so that it hid her face like a veil. "Now all your problems are solved!" she said.

Ellen doubted it, but she realized she couldn't win. "Oh, all right then. But we can't both wear the same costume. I'll have to be a Christmas pudding after all."

Ellen put her finger to her lips as they went downstairs. Mum had invited some of her piano pupils round to play Christmas carols to each other, and at the moment Robert Rumbold was hammering out "Silent Night", though it sounded more like "Very Loud Night".

Katy's house was just round the corner. Her dad opened the door to Ellen and Mirror-Belle.

"Oh good, the food's arrived," he joked when he saw Ellen dressed as a Christmas pudding. "I hope they put a lot of brandy in you." He turned to Mirror-Belle. "And I suppose this delicious-looking white creation is the Christmas cake."

Ellen laughed politely, and then blushed when Mirror-Belle said in a haughty voice, "Please tell the lady of the house that the royal guest has arrived." She seemed to think that she was speaking to the butler.

Luckily Katy's father thought this was a great joke. "Katy! The princess and the pudding are here!" he called out. Then, "If you'll excuse me, I'd better pop upstairs and get changed," he said to Ellen and Mirror-Belle.

"Yes, you do look a bit scruffy. And don't forget to give your shoes a polish while you're at it," said Mirror-Belle.

Before Ellen could tick her off, Katy arrived, dressed as a reindeer.

"I've brought Mirror-Belle with me. I hope that's all right," said Ellen.

"Of course it is." Katy had already met Mirror-Belle once, when she had appeared at their school, and looked pleased to see her again. She took them both into the sitting room, where various children in fancy dress were chattering and eating crisps.

"What an extraordinary-looking tree," said Mirror-Belle. "Why is it growing indoors?"

"It's a Christmas tree," said Ellen.

Mirror-Belle was still bewildered. "What

is this Christmas thing that everyone keeps talking about? Is it some kind of disease?"

Katy laughed. "No, of course not. Why do you think that?"

"Well, that tree looks diseased to me. Half the needles have fallen off it, and the fruits are gleaming in a most unhealthy-looking way. I think you should take it back to the forest immediately."

"They're not fruits, they're fairy lights," said Ellen.

"I think I'm the expert on fairies round here, and I've never heard of such a thing," said Mirror-Belle.

Katy's mother came in. "There's just time for one game before tea," she said.

She handed out pencils and paper and then showed them all a bag. "There are five different things inside here. You'll all get a turn to feel them and then write down what you think they are."

"I can't possibly risk that," objected Mirror-Belle. "Supposing there's something sharp in there? I might prick my finger. But I like the idea of tea. Perhaps you could call one of your servants and ask them to bring me mine while the rest of you play this game."

Katy's mother told her that she would have to wait and have tea with the others. "But I promise you there's nothing sharp in the bag. Why don't you join in?"

Reluctantly Mirror-Belle agreed, though she refused to take her gloves off.

"This is easy," she said when it was her turn to feel inside the bag, and she began writing furiously.

"You can read out your list first if you like, Mirror-Belle," said Katy's mother when everyone was ready.

"Very well," said Mirror-Belle. "There's some mermaid's hair, a wishing ring, an invisibility pill, a witch's eyeball and a tool for removing stones from a unicorn's hoof."

Everyone laughed.

"Very imaginative," said Katy's mum. "I'll give you a mark for the pill, though I don't think it has any magic powers; it's just an ordinary aspirin."

Ellen had written, "seaweed, ring pull from drink can, pill, grape and matchstick", and was delighted to find that she was the only one to get them all right. Her prize was a meringue snowman.

At teatime there were crackers to pull. Mirror-Belle refused to put on the paper crown inside hers and told everyone about the different crowns she had back home.

"Why are you wearing that veil thing?" someone asked.

"It's because my

face is so beautiful that you might fall down dead if you saw it," replied Mirror-Belle. Then she kept them entertained with stories about life in the palace. Ellen was glad that the other children seemed to like Mirror-Belle and think she was fun.

It was after tea that the trouble started. When everyone was back in the sitting room, Katy's mother peeped out the door and announced, "He's coming!"

"Ho ho ho!" came a loud laugh and in strode Father Christmas. Ellen felt quite excited, even though Katy had told her that it was really just her dad dressed up.

"Merry Christmas, boys and girls!" said Father Christmas. "Happy holidays! Ho ho ho!"

"You're extremely late," Mirror-Belle told him. "All the food's gone already."

"Ho ho ho!" laughed Father Christmas, even louder than before.

"What's so funny?" asked Mirror-Belle.

Father Christmas took no notice of her. Still laughing, he heaved the sack off his back. "It's nice to see you all so wide awake!" he told the children. "When I come down your chimneys you're always fast asleep. It gets a bit lonely sometimes."

Mirror-Belle looked even more puzzled. "What do you mean, you come down chimneys? I hope you're not a burglar. We had one of those at the palace once. He stole all the crown jewels. I had to gallop after him on Little Lord Lightning to get them back."

"Ho ho ho!" went Father Christmas, and one or two of the children laughed, but the others said "Shh" or "Shut up".

"Now then." Father Christmas took a

present out of his sack.
"Who's been good all
year?" he asked.

"Me!" everyone
shouted.

He beckoned to a
girl dressed as a star
and she came shyly
forward.

"You look a bit of
a star! Ho ho ho!"
Father Christmas
handed her the present and she unwrapped it. It was a box of soaps shaped
like bells.

"Thank you," said the star girl.

Ellen glanced at Mirror-Belle. She was
still looking suspicious.

Father Christmas gave a torch to a boy
dressed as a cracker, and a card game to
one in a Batman costume.

"Excuse me, but are you quite sure

these things are yours to give away?" Mirror-Belle asked him.

"Ho ho ho," replied Father Christmas, but Ellen didn't think he sounded quite so jolly as before. He beckoned to Mirror-Belle, perhaps hoping that once she had a present of her own she would stop pestering him.

"Now then, Your Royal Highness, let's find something special for you," he said.

Mirror-Belle gave him half a smile. "At least you know how to address me," she said. But when she opened her present her face fell.

"What are these supposed to be?" she asked, looking at the five little felt objects she had unwrapped.

Father Christmas didn't look too sure himself, so Ellen came to the rescue. "They're finger puppets," she said. "A reindeer and a robin and a snowman and a Christmas tree and Father Christmas. They're lovely, aren't they, Mirror-Belle?"

But Mirror-Belle didn't think so. "Is this a trick to get me to take off my gloves?" she asked Father Christmas. "Well, I'm not going to, but I think you should take off your socks and shoes."

"Mirror-Belle! Stop it!" said Ellen, but the Batman boy was intrigued. "Why should he?" he asked.

"They're stolen!" said Mirror-Belle. "They belong to the butler who opened the door."

"There isn't a butler," said someone, and, "She means Katy's dad," said someone else.

"Well, whoever he was, he was wearing scruffy black shoes and socks with green-and-brown diamonds up the sides. Don't you remember, Ellen?" said Mirror-Belle.

"Now, now, you've had your bit of fun," said Father Christmas, covering up his shoes with the hem of his robe and trying to sound jolly again. "Let someone else have a turn, eh? Ho ho ho!"

But Mirror-Belle ignored him. "I see it all now!" she said. "The butler person told Ellen and me he was going upstairs to get changed, and I ordered him to polish his shabby shoes. He must have taken them off, and his socks too. Then I suppose he must have had a little nap, and meanwhile this burglar came down the chimney and stole them."

She turned to Katy's mother. "Aren't you going to phone the police?"

"No," said Katy's mother, "but I think perhaps we'd better phone your parents and tell them you're getting a bit too excited."

"Of course I'm excited!" cried Mirror-Belle. "It's not every day you catch a crook red-handed. Look! He's even got a false beard!" She reached out and tried to tug it, but Father Christmas dodged out of the way.

"Now now, I'm beginning to wonder if you really are a good little girl," he said. "Maybe I'd better fill your stocking with coal instead of presents?"

Mirror-Belle looked horrified. "You're not filling any of my stockings with anything!" she said. "In fact, if you come anywhere near the palace I'll set my dog, Prince Precious Paws, on you. And you'd better not try going down my friend Ellen's chimney either."

"Of course I'll go down Ellen's chimney; she's a good girl, and I've got a little something for her here," said Father Christmas, beckoning to Ellen.

Ellen came up to receive her present. "Do calm down, Mirror-Belle," she pleaded.

"I know!" said Katy. "We're going to play hide-and-seek next. Why don't you

*
* 401 *

go and hide now, Mirror-Belle? I bet you'll find a really good place."

Mirror-Belle sighed. "Very well, since no one here will listen to reason," she said, and she flounced out of the room.

Later, when all the presents had been given out and Father Christmas had said goodbye, the other children went to look for Mirror-Belle. Ellen was not surprised when they couldn't find her.

"It's all right," she told Katy's mum. "I think she must have gone home. She quite often does that." She didn't add that the way Mirror-Belle went home was through a mirror.

Ellen thought she would never get to sleep. Christmas Eve was always like that. Her empty stocking (really one of Dad's thick mountain-climbing socks) lay limply on the bottom of her bed. In the morning it would be fat and knobbly with presents, and this was just one of the exciting thoughts that was keeping her awake.

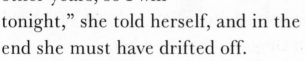

"But I did get to sleep all the other years, so I will tonight," she told herself, and in the end she must have drifted off.

A rapping sound woke her and she sat up in bed. The room was dark. It was still night.

She wriggled her toes. Yes! From the lovely heaviness on top of them she knew that her stocking was full. But why was her heart thumping so hard? It didn't feel just like nice Christmassy excitement. That noise had scared her. What was it?

Mum and Dad liked Ellen to take her stocking into their room, so that they could watch her open it. This year she had decided to take them in a cup of tea as well. But somehow she knew it was too early for that. She switched on her lamp and looked at the clock beside her bed. Only four thirty.

Suddenly she heard another rap. It was coming from the skylight window. Ellen wished now that Mirror-Belle hadn't gone on about burglars so much, because that was the first thing she thought of. It sounded as if someone was trying to break into her bedroom.

"Ellen! Let me in!"

That hoarse whisper didn't belong to a burglar. It was Princess Mirror-Belle.

For once Ellen was relieved to see her face, which was pressed against the sky-light window.

"I'm coming!" she said and got out of bed.

The window was in the sloping part of

Ellen's ceiling, where it came down so low that grown-ups couldn't stand up properly. Ellen didn't even need to climb on a chair to open it.

Princess Mirror-Belle landed on the floor with a thump. She didn't look much like Sleeping Beauty any more. Her face was dirty, her hair wild and her nightdress torn. In one hand she clutched the now grubby veil.

"Mirror-Belle! I thought you'd gone back through one of Katy's mirrors!"

"What, and leave you unprotected? Is that the kind of friend you think I am?"

"I don't know what you mean. Oh, Mirror-Belle, you're shivering! Why don't you get into my bed?"

"That's a good idea."

When the two girls were sitting up in bed together, snugly covered by Ellen's duvet, Ellen said, "What were you doing on the roof? And how did you get there?"

"I climbed up that creeper at the side of your house. Very useful things, creepers. I'm sure my friend Rapunzel wishes that there had been one growing up the tower that horrible witch locked her up in for all those years. Then the prince could have climbed up that instead of up her hair. I must say, I wouldn't let any old prince climb up my hair, even if it was long enough. A lot of Rapunzel's hair fell out after that, you know, and it's never been the same since."

"Oh, Mirror-Belle, do stop going on about Rapunzel and tell me what you've been up to."

"This," said Mirror-Belle, and she spread out the grubby veil which she had been clutching. Something was written on it in big black letters.

"I had to use a lump of coal for the writing, but it looks quite good, I think. Don't you?"

Ellen had become an expert at reading Mirror-Belle's writing so she didn't need to hold it up to the mirror to see that it said, "Go Away, Father Christmas".

"I spread it out on the roof and sat on the chimney pot all night," said Mirror-Belle triumphantly. "I'm pretty sure that's done the trick. I don't think he'll come now."

"Er . . . " Ellen couldn't help glancing down at the bulgy stocking on her bed, and Mirror-Belle spotted it too.

"Good heavens! He's craftier than I thought. How on earth did he get in? You'd better check all your belongings immediately, Ellen, and see what he's stolen."

"I'm sure he hasn't stolen anything," said Ellen.

Mirror-Belle glanced round the room suspiciously and then at the stocking again.

"I notice there isn't one for me," she said. "That's a relief," she added, though in fact she sounded rather disappointed.

Ellen thought quickly and then said, "I've got something for you, Mirror-Belle. Close your eyes a minute."

Mirror-Belle looked pleased, and Ellen hastily wrapped up the present that Father Christmas had given her at Katy's party.

"You can open them again now."

Mirror-Belle unwrapped the present, and gazed in delight at the little glass dome with a forest scene of deer and trees inside it.

"Give it a shake," said Ellen. Mirror-

Belle shook it, and snow-flakes rose up and whirled around.

"This is just what I've always wanted," she said. Ellen had never heard her sound so 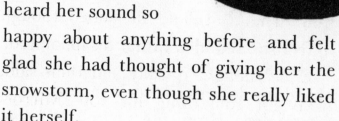 happy about anything before and felt glad she had thought of giving her the snowstorm, even though she really liked it herself.

After a few more shakes and smiles, Mirror-Belle started eyeing Ellen's stocking again. "I hope it isn't full of coal," she said.

"I'm sure it's not."

"Let's just check."

"But I usually open it in Mum and Dad's room, and it's too early to wake them."

"I still think we have a duty to investigate," said Mirror-Belle grandly.

"Well . . . " Ellen was beginning to waver. After all, it was so hard to wait. "I know, let's just open one thing each and then wrap them up again."

She gave Mirror-Belle a cube-shaped parcel and unwrapped a long thin one herself.

"Cool! It's a fan. What's in yours?"

"It's a little box." Mirror-Belle opened it and inside was a brooch shaped like a Scottie dog. "Hmm, not a patch on any of my own jewellery, but quite amusing all the same," she said. "Would you like me to fasten it on to your pyjama top?"

"Yes, please," said Ellen.

Suddenly Mirror-Belle gave a little scream.

"What's the matter?"

"I've pricked my finger!"

"Oh dear." Ellen looked at the finger which was sticking out of a hole in the dirty white glove. She couldn't see any blood or even a pinprick. "I'm sure you'll be all right," she said.

"No, I won't. I feel sleepy already."

"Oh help! Is there anything I can do?"

"No, nothing at all, but don't worry. It's quite a nice feeling actually. In fact, I think I probably *need* a three-hundred-year sleep after all the adventures I've had recently."

Mirror-Belle gave a huge yawn and lay down in Ellen's bed.

"No! You can't go to sleep here!"

But Mirror-Belle's eyes were already closed, and she began to snore gently.

"Wake up, Mirror-Belle!" Ellen was shouting now.

"Ellen! What's going on!" she heard her mother's voice call.

Ellen looked at the clock. It was half past five – still a bit earlier than her parents liked to be disturbed, but it seemed that she had woken them up already.

Well, she decided, at least now she could prove to them once and for all that Mirror-Belle really existed. If she was going to stay asleep in Ellen's bed for three hundred years there could be no doubt about that.

"Happy Christmas," said Mum sleepily, and then, "Oh, how lovely," when she saw that Ellen had brought her and Dad a cup of tea.

"Where's your stocking?" asked Dad.

"It's upstairs still, and so is Mirror-Belle! You've got to come and see her."

Mum sighed. "Honestly, Ellen, can't

we even get a break from Mirror-Belle on Christmas Day?"

"But she's asleep in my bed! Please, Mum – please come!"

Mum yawned. "Let us drink our tea first," she said. "You go back up and we'll come in a couple of minutes."

"All right." After all, Ellen thought, there was no hurry.

But when she got back to her bedroom she found that Mirror-Belle was no longer in the bed. She was walking slowly across the room with her arms stretched out in front of her.

"Mirror-Belle! Have you woken up already?"

"No, of course not, silly. I'm sleepwalking," said Mirror-Belle. Ellen noticed that she was grasping the snowstorm in her right hand. She had reached the wardrobe now.

"Goodbye, Ellen," she said in a strange

calm voice and disappeared into the mirror.

"Mirror-Belle! Come back!" Ellen called into the mirror, but it was her own reflection and not Mirror-Belle that she saw there.

"All right then, where's this sleeping princess?" said Dad, coming into the room with Mum.

"You've just missed her," said Ellen. "She's sleepwalked into the mirror."

"Well, well, what a surprise," said Mum. Then she glanced at the wrapping paper on the bed. "I see you couldn't wait to start opening your stocking."

"That was Mirror-Belle's idea," said Ellen.

Mum smiled. "Of course," she said.

Ellen knew that Mum and Dad didn't believe her. It was annoying, but she didn't really blame them. There were quite a few things about Mirror-Belle that she wasn't sure if she believed herself. For instance, had she really gone to sleep for three hundred years? If so, Ellen would never see her again – unless she did some more sleepwalking, that is.

"Well," said Mum, "are you going to bring your stocking downstairs now?"

"Yes," said Ellen. Suddenly she felt excited all over again.

Mirror-Belle had gone, but Christmas Day had only just begun.

PLAY TIME

Julia Donaldson

A wicked wolf on the prowl
Two clever crooks in search of loot
A beautiful girl imprisoned in the underworld

From traditional to modern, from fantasy to fun, there's a part for everyone in this brilliant collection of eleven short plays written by bestselling author Julia Donaldson.

Perfect for primary-school or family use, and suitable for a wide variety of ages and abilities, *Play Time* provides everything the budding actor needs to raise the curtain on the wonderful world of theatre!

Ballerina Stories

Illustrated by Lara Jones

Chosen by Emma Young

You'll find some magical ballet shoes, a couple of Nutcrackers, one or two fairy ballerinas . . . and plenty of twinkling tutus!

A beautiful collection of stories by Julia Donaldson, Anna Wilson, Fiona Dunbar and many other top children's writers.

Pirouette your way through the pages!

Puppy Love

By Anna Wilson

I, Summer Holly Love, have wished a million thousand times for a puppy of my own, for ever and ever, AMEN.

So I was over the top of the moon with happiness when I finally obtained Parental Consent to get Honey – the most absolutely softest and velvetest puppy in the whole world. Although being a pet owner is not the most easiest trick in the book. Honey and I have had some Extremely Entertaining adventures together. (Like the time we had to deal with my weird sister April's cringesome love crush on Honey's vet . . .)

The first hilarious, slightly barking mad book about Summer and Honey

A selected list of titles available fro...
Macmillan Children's Books

The prices shown below are correct at the time of going to press. However, Macmillan Publishers reserves the right to show new retail prices on covers, which may differ from those previously advertised.

Julia Donaldson

Crazy Mayonnaisy Mum	978-0-330-41490-6	£3.99
Play Time	978-0-330-44595-5	£4.99

Chosen by Emma Young

Ballerina Stories	978-0-330-45273-1	£4.99

Anna Wilson

Puppy Love	978-0-330-45289-2	£4.99

All Pan Macmillan titles can be ordered from our website, www.panmacmillan.com, or from your local bookshop and are also available by post from:

Bookpost, PO Box 29, Douglas, Isle of Man IM99 1BQ

Credit cards accepted. For details:
Telephone: 01624 677237
Fax: 01624 670923
Email: bookshop@enterprise.net
www.bookpost.co.uk

Free postage and packing in the United Kingdom